C9

D0522607

THE TWISTED TONGUES

A wartime traitor who broadcast from Germany is finally released from prison. Nobody wanted to listen to him during the war and nobody wants to listen to him now. But he intends to be heard, and when he begins to write his memoirs for a newspaper, old ghosts stir uneasily and it becomes a race against time: will he reveal the truth behind the smug respectability of men in high places before they find a means of silencing him forever?

Books by John Burke
in the Linford Mystery Library:

JOHN BURKE

THE TWISTED TONGUES

Complete and Unabridged

LINFORD
Leicester

First published in Great Britain

First Linford Edition
published 2013

A catalogue record for this book is available
from the British Library.

ISBN 978–1–4448–1760–7

Published by
F. A. Thorpe (Publishing)
Anstey, Leicestershire

Set by Words & Graphics Ltd.
Anstey, Leicestershire
Printed and bound in Great Britain by
T. J. International Ltd., Padstow, Cornwall

This book is printed on acid-free paper

For
HARRY RABINOWITZ
who
added so much

Can honour's voice
  provoke the silent dust . . . ?
                —*Thomas Gray*

1

Echoes of Treason

1

On a misty morning in early October two men stood by a window of their club. They were both in their middle sixties, both drinking pink gins, and both contemplating murder, though neither wished to be the first to put this into words.

Below the window the traffic pulsed insistently. On the far side of the road the trees were beginning to shed their leaves. Feet and tyres lifted the dry, curled fragments and kept them moving for a while until eventually they all settled in the gutters. Autumn was late and leisurely.

Every now and then a surge of conversation in the bar drowned the remorseless throbbing outside. When Charles Tenby walked in he felt momentarily reassured by the warmth and familiarity of the place. The curtains needed cleaning; the armchair in the far corner still squealed protestingly when a heavy man slumped into it; the cartoons of past members went on yellowing away behind their glass. It was all as safe and comforting as it had always been. Safe . . . until that day last week when Philip Sengall came out into the world once more.

Tenby approached his two friends near the window. General Henstock's aggressively sandy head was thrown back as he looked up at Lord Robsart, massive and imposing against the light.

The general was saying: 'And you haven't heard from him?'

'Not yet,' said Robsart. 'He hasn't approached me personally, anyway. My editor's looking for him, to get an interview — but so is every other paper in Fleet Street. They all want to know what he's got to say for himself.'

He lowered his voice as Tenby came up, then nodded a welcome as he saw who it was.

Tenby said: 'Perhaps he won't have anything at all to say. He's got nothing to gain.'

'Except money,' grunted Henstock.

'Blackmail?'

'Wouldn't put it past him.'

'It's not in keeping with his character,' said Tenby. He saw Henstock scowl. With no effort at all he had always been able to irritate the general. He went on: 'When Frodsham saw him last night — '

'He went to Frodsham?'

Tenby had been looking forward to the sight of their faces when he told them. Dangerous as the whole affair could be, he still preferred to treat it as a game for as long as possible. The serious thinking would come soon enough.

'Frodsham telephoned me this morning,' he said. 'Apparently they sat up until the small hours while Sengall unburdened himself. It would seem that our old colleague doesn't trust us nowadays.'

'Fifteen years,' snapped Henstock. 'Preyed on his mind. Given him delusions.'

They all three knew that there was no

question of delusions.

'He wrote me several letters from prison,' Robsart said, 'picking on recent editorials in my papers and asking what was behind them.'

'As far as I could make out from Frodsham's account,' said Tenby, remembering Frodsham's high, wandering voice in his ear, 'Sengall suggests that if we are still true — and Frodsham couldn't make out what he meant by that — there ought to be room for him somewhere. He told Frodsham that he still has a lot to say.'

'Just what I told you,' said Henstock: 'money.'

Tenby shook his head. 'Money was not mentioned.'

'Not directly, maybe.'

'The man made no threats. He simply appeared to regard it as a duty on our part. We have prospered while he suffered in gaol for his principles — that's roughly the approach. And Frodsham seems to sympathize with him.'

'Fancy going to that doddering old idiot first.'

'He was the one,' Tenby recalled, 'to

whom we all went in the early days. He was the one who held us together.'

'Can't even hold himself together today,' snorted Henstock. Then he said: 'Is Sengall still there — still up in Cambridge?'

'No. Frodsham said he left early this morning. He can hardly have had a wink of sleep.'

'Done enough sleeping these fifteen years, I suppose.' Henstock drained his glass and then realized that Tenby was not yet drinking. 'Sorry. The usual?' He went to the bar.

The other two were silent for a moment. Tenby looked out over the park to the tower of Big Ben rising beyond the flushed autumnal trees. Automatically his left hand went up to his lapel. One day there would be a cartoon of him standing like this, a cartoon darkening in one of those frames on the wall. He was a well-known feature of the club, standing at this window with his gaze remotely but possessively fixed on the Houses of Parliament: he knew it, knew that they laughed, but knew also that the laughter was more than half envious and that he was regarded as a success. Which, indeed, he was. There had been some tricky moments, but he had made the right decisions at the right times and now he was a man to be reckoned with.

'How's the family?' asked Robsart.

'Fine, thanks.'

'The boy's going up to King's this term?'

'That's right. And Molly is expecting to make me a grandfather before Christmas.'

He checked his enthusiasm for the people he loved. Robsart did not really expect to be answered in detail unless the question were political or financial.

'You've done very nicely,' said Robsart distantly.

Very nicely, thought Tenby. Nothing could pull him down now. Even Sengall could surely not do any real damage. But at the back of his mind was a sharp-edged fear. Sengall had not been like the rest of them. Sengall was a fanatic; and there was no telling what fanatics would do.

It would be much better if Sengall ceased to exist.

6

That was as far as Tenby allowed himself to go in his own mind. Just that the man should somehow cease to exist.

He wished Robsart would do something about it. Or Henstock, who had been ruthless enough in the North African campaign and who showed up in a pretty lurid light in the wartime memoirs of other generals. Let one of them take action — and soon.

General Henstock came back with three glasses. He said: 'Did he leave any address with Frodsham?'

'None.'

'There's not much we can do,' said Robsart, 'until he shows up again.'

'And then?' said Henstock.

'Then . . . ' Robsart drank thoughtfully. 'There are only six of us left. And two we can rule out as being senile. They're not to be relied on.'

Henstock jabbed his left arm out stiffly and looked at his watch. 'Better get a bite to eat before all the tables are grabbed.' And as they finished their drinks and moved towards the door he said: 'I wonder who he'll tackle next? Braith-waite, perhaps. Or one of us.'

'If he shows up at all,' said Tenby.

'He'll show up,' said Henstock, 'sooner or later. And wherever it is, it'll mean trouble.'

As they approached the dining-room door Tenby fell back a few paces. He sensed that the other two were going to say something of which he approved but which he preferred not to hear. Let them find a way of doing what had to be done; let him not be drawn in.

But the distance was not great enough. He heard.

'Perhaps we can make him see reason,' Robsart was saying. 'He's a beaten man. There won't be any real fight left in him. We can laugh him off' — there was no laughter in his words — 'or frighten him into keeping his mouth shut.'

'There's only one sure way of shutting mouths,' said Henstock.

'Until we've been in touch with him we can't be sure — '

'For myself,' said Henstock, 'I really don't think we can afford to let him live.'

2

Leonard, the First Baron Robsart, had a small house in Scotland, a large flat in Park Street, and an estate in Gloucester which his wife had brought to him on their marriage. She preferred to stay in Gloucester, so he drove down there at weekends. As a rule he invited a dozen people one week-end in each month. His invitations were coveted and at the same time dreaded. He was aware that even a Cabinet Minister liked to say, after reading a *Courier* editorial: 'That's exactly what Robsart was saying last Sunday when I was down at his place — I thought then that he was bound to get one of his chaps to develop the theme.'

In London he dined out a great deal but liked to keep a certain number of evenings free. He liked the calm of his flat with the Munnings over the fireplace, the Paoletti portrait of himself on the facing wall, the bookcases, and the bottle at his elbow. Alone, he felt more content with his achievements than when there were other people there to sing his praises.

That October evening after meeting Henstock and Tenby he had eaten well and was settled with a book due for publication a fortnight from now. Tenby had written his memoirs and would undoubtedly expect a wide spread of reviews in the Robsart newspapers. Robsart was not sure that he approved of Tenby writing his memoirs, and proposed to vet them before letting the reviewer get at them. Perhaps he would write something himself: he liked to contribute the occasional feature, secure in the knowledge that it would be neither rejected nor tampered with by the editor.

There was a tap at the door. Craddock came in, bowing slightly in that way of his which was melancholy rather than servile.

'There is a Mr Sengall here, sir. I told him you would not wish to be disturbed, but he appears to think — '

'Show him in.' Robsart sat very still. 'And as soon as you have done that, Craddock, telephone General Henstock and tell him that . . . that Mr Sengall is here. Just that.'

He got up and stood before the fireplace. Light gleamed on the flanks of the mare in the painting. From across the room his own face stared at him. The eyes were very blue and he had had more hair then, ten years ago.

Sengall came in. Craddock shut the door soundlessly behind him.

Robsart said with difficulty: 'Good evening, Philip.'

'Fancy your remembering my name.'

'Oh, come now, my dear chap.'

'You and the others seem to have forgotten so many things very happily.'

He had always had a flat voice but now it was utterly dead. It lacked the hypnotic rasp that had once come so derisively from so many radio receivers.

'Do sit down,' said Robsart.

Instead of doing so, Sengall put his hands behind his back and went on a tour of inspection of the room. He stopped for a long time before the Paoletti.

'An excellent likeness,' he said. 'You haven't changed. A little fatter in the face, perhaps. But you always did well for yourself, didn't you? The real changes took place long ago — and they happened inside, not on the surface.'

He had always been small and now he looked shrunken. It was as though he had huddled away inside himself to shelter from the humiliations of the last fifteen years. Now that he was free he was still unable to stand upright. When he blinked, his eyelids closed and opened in a dreamy fashion like those of some drowsy bird. His nose, too, was like a bird's — a small, emaciated beak.

'Do sit down,' said Robsart again.

Sengall appeared to debate this silently and then chose a chair on the other side of the fireplace. It was a large chair that swallowed him up. There was so little of him, and what there was appeared so insignificant. He was one of those destined for defeat. He had chosen wrongly and this was what it had done to him.

Abruptly he said: 'I've seen Frodsham.'

'So I hear.'

'So he's been in touch with you? I wouldn't have thought he mixed with you nowadays. He never let go of the truth, the way you did. He never betrayed our cause.'

'None of us betrayed the cause.' The words were stilted and absurd. Robsart had never had any time for slogans in his personal life and conversation. If they were useful in his newspapers he did not stand in the way of their use. 'Look,' he said reasonably, 'we're sorry you had to go through what you did . . . but you acted rather impulsively, dashing off the way you did. One has to . . . well . . . adjust to circumstances.'

'Is that what you're doing now?' demanded Sengall with sudden vigour. 'Is that why you're making your papers say what they say, and why Tenby is up on his feet in Parliament telling the country what I told it years ago, when nobody would listen? Why now, when you kept so quiet for so long? Adjusting to circumstances, you call it. Opportunism might be a better description.'

Robsart said coldly: 'Coming from the one who sent that letter, I think such a comment is a trifle grotesque.'

Sengall, hunched in his chair, shook

his head in wonderment. 'You really think . . . ?'

'You're not trying to claim you know nothing about it?

'It was one of *you*,' said Sengall in his deathly flat voice. 'I still want to know which. I'm the only one who never turned traitor.'

It was ludicrous that this man should utter the word with such conviction. But in his own warped way it was plain that he believed what he was saying. Small as he was, he would have to be crushed.

Robsart said: 'Why have you come to see me?'

'I have been wondering about you. I wonder if you are now on the right side for the right reasons. The truth should be spoken aloud. I want to find some way of making people understand. If you're sincere this time you need me. I want to tell people my life story and let them see how I worked to stop the world reaching the state it is in today.'

Robsart nodded. Perhaps there was still a way of getting round this without violence. He said: 'The *Courier* pays well for exclusive material. We could run a short serial, ghosted by one of my staff.'

'I would prefer to write it myself.' Sengall's eyes were fixed not on Robsart but on some inner truth. 'I must speak before it is too late. And I don't think you are really interested. How can you be sincere when you denied everything for so long?' He began to push himself up out of the embrace of the chair. 'You don't want me in on it this time, do you? It would be too embarrassing. I made a mistake in coming here — I can see it.'

Outside a car purred to a halt. It was a frequent enough sound, but in this case there was something unusual. Nobody got out. Whoever had driven up was sitting in the car, waiting.

'Where are you living?' asked Robsart.

'Living?' Sengall's whisper was full of mockery. 'I have not begun to live again. Not yet. I am staying somewhere unpretentious. Yes. Since there is so little to which I can pretend.'

He was moving towards the door.

Robsart said tensely: 'What happened to the papers?'

'Papers?'

'Our records. Our files. Did you take them all with you or were they — are they — hidden away somewhere in England?'

'Oh, you fool,' said Sengall with incredible mildness.

Robsart pressed the bell-push by the fireplace. 'It's all over now,' he said. 'You can speak. You can admit what happened. What did become of them in the end?'

'You really think I was the one?'

'It's a bit pointless to keep up this pretence after all these years.'

'You fool,' said Sengall again.

Craddock came into the room. Robsart said: 'Show this gentleman out, will you, Craddock?' He put out his hand. Sengall's fingers were very cold. Craddock held the door open and Sengall went out. The door closed behind them. Robsart turned away and switched off the light beside the fireplace. Then he crossed to the window and drew back the curtain.

The car was dark black, its roof and bonnet gleaming under the street lamp. It was parked ten yards away, facing north.

Downstairs the front door opened. A

faint haze of light flowed across the pavement. Sengall stepped out and began to walk away. The light was soaked up by the shadow of the door swinging across it and closing.

The black car coughed gently into life and moved forward, hugging the pavement.

Sengall glanced over his shoulder. The slowness of it and the way it clung to the kerb must have triggered off a swift suspicion. He began to walk more quickly and then burst into a run.

Robsart lost sight of him. Standing at the window and trying to see along the street he could follow only the relentless car.

The car stopped. The nearside front door opened and a man stumbled out. He plunged across the pavement and then came back into view, holding Sengall with one hand and beating him across the face with the other. The two of them fell against the car. An arm reached out from within to get a grip on Sengall. The little man ducked and for a moment was free; then his captor pounced again.

Suddenly the whole scene was brightly illuminated. The headlights of a car swinging in from Upper Brook Street picked out the struggling figures. The driver, presumably unnerved by the unexpected vision of violence, stabbed on his horn and kept up a wild trumpeting as he came nearer.

Sengall lashed out. The arm from within reached for him again, got a purchase, and drew him halfway into the front seat. The other car closed in, still bellowing. Sengall wrenched himself free and the door of the car slammed shut. From where Robsart stood with his cheek against the cold glass of the window it looked as though Sengall's wrist were trapped. Abruptly he reeled backwards and disappeared. The car pulled away from the pavement. As it gathered speed the door opened once more, a dark shape sprang in and pulled it shut, and there was a roar of acceleration.

Robsart let the curtain fall.

Thirty minutes later his telephone rang. He knew as he lifted the receiver who it would be.

General Henstock said: 'He got away.'

'So I gathered.'

'He's still quite a fighter.' There was reluctant admiration in the general's voice. 'He hasn't forgotten some of the tricks he learnt in that place along the King's Road. Anyway . . . What did he have to say?'

'From now on I think he'll be a menace. He knows too much about the past and he's shrewd enough to guess accurately about the present. If only you'd been able to get your hands on him!'

'We'll find him,' said Henstock. 'One thing I can tell you, anyway: my men say they winged him. Quite a mess, they think. His right hand won't be in any condition for writing nasty letters to your paper or any other paper for some time.'

Robsart said: 'He can always dictate them.'

3

Nora Downing rarely bought an evening paper on her way home. Her uncle always had the final edition of his own paper and those of his rivals on the coffee table by the time she got there. Occasionally she glimpsed a headline over someone's shoulder and spent the fifteen minutes between her office and home speculating what it meant or what the Evan Downing policy with regard to it would be.

This evening she saw the entire front page of the paper on a news-seller's orange box. The right-hand column was devoted to an announcement in heavy black type of a serial starting in the *Sunday Mercury*: 'THE TRUTH BEHIND THE TREACHERY, by Philip Sengall'.

She supposed it was a scoop. Her uncle would make it seem so, anyway. Nora did not feel that the memoirs of a wartime traitor would be either savoury or interesting so many years after. But Uncle Evan usually knew what he was doing. Even if it was only to score off Lord Robsart there would have been a good reason for his action.

Twilight was smoky in the Kensington streets as she arrived home. One side of Viscount's Gate was pale with a remote, diffused light. The slope rising to the park faded away into a distant world.

Before she had closed the front door her uncle was crossing the hall to meet her.

'There you are, my dear.'

She put up her face to be kissed. His hard, dry mouth brushed across her cheek. Then he put his arm across her shoulders and marched rather than led her into his study.

'What does it feel like to be free?' he asked.

'It's a bit early to say.'

She had just left her job in a public relations group which was expanding too rapidly by means which she found too unscrupulous. She was not yet sure that she had done the right thing, but when she made the decision a fortnight ago it had been inevitable. Today had been her last day, and all the people in the organization whom she had thought most unlikeable had been charming and very human. But she couldn't have stayed on.

'You'll soon be clamouring for slavery once more,' said her uncle. 'But don't go rushing into things again. Take it easy for a few weeks.'

Uncle Evan had asked for no explanations, no details. Perhaps he had felt that the things she disliked in public relations would be too uncomfortably close to the things from which he made his living in the newspaper world. Or perhaps, as usual, he was wary of coming too close. Here he was, at this moment, smiling affectionately at her; but there was a warning in the smile. Don't overdo it, he was saying. His whole manner had always said this. The editors and staff of his papers were encouraged to overdo absolutely everything: there were no limitations, no holds barred. But in private life he was wary of emotion and even of ordinary friendliness.

Evan Downing had ensured a good but practical education for his niece. Her parents had been killed in an air raid when she was five and after that he had made himself responsible for her. Three successive housekeepers had taken her under their wing but had not been allowed to spoil her or become too possessive. Downing was suspicious of demonstrative warmth in human relationships. He was a Welshman who had made a fortune out of the newspaper empire which he had built up in just over thirty years. He was unmarried, having never met a woman as forceful and direct as himself. He regarded himself as a matter-of-fact 'man of the people' but did not recognize in himself — as Nora had recognized from an early age — a strain of Welsh imagination and poetry. He was a materialistic mystic, a hard-headed romantic. She did not doubt that he loved her but sometimes she felt that it was an orderly, well-defined love that would never conflict with his other interests.

Now he said: 'We have a guest for dinner this evening.'

'Anybody interesting?'

'Very interesting.'

She would have preferred a quiet evening, a chance to unwind after the uncertainties of the day; but she could tell that he would be disappointed if she pleaded a headache or tiredness. He took it for granted that things would happen the way he wanted them to happen. They rarely failed him.

'Who is it?' she asked.

Before he could answer, the telephone rang. He picked it up, listened, then said: 'Already? Not wasting any time, are they? . . . No. Did you get a description of him? . . . Mm. Could be anybody. Not that it makes any difference. Well, don't give them a lead. Tell them to read the *Sunday Mercury*.'

Knowing him, she suddenly knew who the guest was. As he replaced the receiver she said: 'Philip Sengall is dining with us, then?'

Downing chuckled. 'You saw the announcement?' Then the amusement ebbed away. 'But if you jumped to it as quickly as that there'll be others. They've been asking questions at the office. Next thing they'll be planted out there in the street, waiting. Or not waiting.' He glanced at his watch. 'Well, you'll be wanting to change, I expect.'

It was his usual formal dismissal. He had work to do — most of it consisting of looking for faults in his own paper and for good things in the rival papers so that he could telephone his editor and raise hell. He was not concerned with what Nora did for the next couple of hours. She could sit in her room, have a bath, or go for a long walk. She was a free agent. But he would want her to be there at the end of those two hours to talk to him and listen to him; or just, at any rate, to be there.

She had a leisurely bath and changed into her dark blue dress. Then she spent an hour with a novel open on her knee, not reading. Vaguely she speculated about the sort of job she would like to do next. Even more vaguely she wondered what sort of people she would meet next time. Inevitably there would be another Simon, another Bill — the eager young men who wanted her to be something closer and more intimate than a colleague, and couldn't understand why she was not interested in them.

She did not really understand this herself.

'What are you waiting for?' Simon had once demanded, angrily. 'You say there's nobody else — never has been anybody else. So what the hell are you waiting for: old age?'

Nora had no idea what she was waiting for. She simply knew that it had not yet arrived. The Simons and Bills and Martins came, cavorted around her for a while, and then drifted away into forgetfulness. Some of them got hurt, but it was none of her doing.

'You're a cold bitch. Cold through and through.' It was Martin who had said that, trying to hurt her in return. She had felt too sorry for him to be upset. Every now and then she wondered if the accusation was true, but without any real alarm.

At last she went downstairs. The study door was open. The light on the desk was on and the electric fire glowed in the grate. Nora went in and opened the corner cupboard. She poured herself a dry sherry.

The light fell on the photographs of herself that stood side by side on her uncle's desk. There was one of her at the age of seven and one taken on her twenty-first birthday. The child was a stranger, shadowy-eyed and wistful; the young woman even more a stranger. Nora could not accept that picture of herself. In the mirror she saw herself always in motion, cleaning her teeth or setting her hair or putting lipstick on. She never sat and contemplated her own face just for the sake of it. In the photograph she was frozen. Her eyes were level and unyielding, her mouth slightly scornful, her hair very dark and brilliant against the background. Uncle Evan assured her that it was an excellent likeness, but she did not recognize the imprisoned face and felt that he must have very little idea of what she was really like.

Voices came across the hall and into the room. Nora turned towards them.

As her uncle introduced her to the hunched little man he had brought in, she put out her right hand before noticing that the visitor's hand was swathed in bandages. When she substituted her left hand he gripped it hard as though to establish that he was a man to be reckoned with and in no need of pity. His pallor was frightening.

At dinner Sengall drank his soup with difficulty, balancing the spoon awkwardly in his left hand. Downing did not notice. Nora, after a couple of minutes, said: 'If you'd like me to get a cup instead . . . '

'Thank you. I'll manage.'

But when the maid brought in the roast lamb, Downing cut Sengall's helping into manageable pieces without discussing the matter.

Conversation was stilted. For Nora there was no possible starting point. What did you say politely to a man who had deserted his country, broadcast for the enemy, skulked in hiding for years, and just emerged from fifteen years of imprisonment? Even if you accepted that the punishment had wiped out the crime it was difficult to think up conventional phrases and small talk. Before the meal was halfway over Downing made it clear that he had no intention of trying. He proposed to plunge straight into the reality of it all. He said:

'Now. Let's get things worked out.'

'It is all straightforward,' said Sengall.

'Not to Nora. She doesn't know the programme yet. But I think you'll agree that she is the right person for the job.'

Sengall looked at Nora. His expression did not change.

Nora said: 'What job?'

'We need someone absolutely reliable to act as Mr Sengall's secretary for the next few weeks,' said her uncle.

'Oh, but — '

'His story is to appear in the *Sunday Mercury*. The instalments are going to be carefully planned, building up from the basic facts to some interesting revelations that will rock this country. A lot of distinguished heads are going to fall. We can't afford a leak before publication. No ordinary shorthand typist will do. Even our most trusted girls on the paper might blab. They have homes and boy friends.'

'And lives of their own,' said Nora. She was caught up in a surge of resentment. He had made all his plans before she even got home today. She was just a part of his empire — one of his vassals, expected to jump when he cracked the whip.

Downing frowned at her with dark Celtic reproach. 'You've not lacked for freedom, girl.'

'Freedom,' she said, 'under the protective umbrella of Downing Publications. And umbrellas cast shadows.'

Sengall glanced inscrutably from one to the other.

Evan Downing said: 'I particularly want you to do this for me, Nora. I've simply got to have someone I can trust. It won't be a long business. But it's an important one. There are plenty of men who will want to stop us if they can, using any means they can — men you probably think of as pillars of English society, defenders of the English way of life. But when the pillars are cracked right through, when the defenders have long ago been seduced from their loyalties by money and the promise of power . . . then the truth must be told. It's the duty of the Press to see that it's told. I need your help, Nora.'

She thought abstractedly that with that musical frenzy in his voice he ought to have been a revivalist preacher. Perhaps in a way, as a newspaper tycoon, he was just that.

She said: 'If influential people are involved, the libel laws — '

'I'll attend to that part of it. I know exactly how to handle the leakage of names and information. And I've had my own ideas about some of those names for many years past. Mr Sengall's job is to tell what he knows; your job is to get it down on paper for me.'

In Sengall's presence she could hardly express the instinctive distaste she felt for him. In fighting off the job that her uncle was thrusting on her she had to use lame excuses. 'I was hoping to have a few days' holiday.'

'When the job is over you can have a long holiday. I promise. Anywhere you like. The South of France, Majorca, the Bahamas . . . name it.'

Sengall himself unexpectedly intervened in little more than a whisper. His voice crawled into her ears like a rustling, probing insect. He said:

'I don't think I have a lot of time. I would like to say what must be said before they reach me. It has always been a surprise to me that they did not find a way of getting at me in prison and finishing the job there. It is easy enough, in prison.'

'Not in England,' said Downing.

'No? Then English prisons must be very different from all others.'

'You should be the expert on that.' It was as though Downing had only just realized what species of creature he was dealing with — a strange sort of man to be sitting at his dinner table. Brusquely he went on: 'Anyway, it's up to you how you put your story across. Tell it the way it comes, and leave the rest to us. My staff will tidy up the loose ends afterwards. And I promise you that they will not tamper with the meaning of what you say. I suggest' — it was a command rather than a suggestion — 'you use the small room at the back of the house. It's quieter there. You can start first thing tomorrow morning. Ought to be able to get the basic material of the first instalment down in a day or two.'

Downing set to work on his food again with renewed appetite. They finished the meal in a silence which was broken only as coffee was brought in. Then Downing laughed.

'This is going to make old Robsart sit up!'

'Indeed it is,' Sengall agreed softly.

4

In spite of her doubts and her repugnance for the whole idea Nora did not lie awake in any ferment of irritation. She slept well and came downstairs at the usual time for breakfast. Sengall was there, shrunken and out of place in this familiar room. She wondered whether he had lain awake last night shaping phrases and circumlocutions in his mind.

As soon as breakfast was finished her uncle said boisterously: 'Well, I'll leave you to it. See if you can break the back of it today.'

Sengall gave an odd little giggle. 'It's a long time since I broke any backs.'

The dictation session started laboriously. Sengall had once been a fluent speaker, but there was a difference between making propagandist speeches and dictating a coherent narrative. Instead of outlining the essential facts he began to explain reasons and motives and ways of justifying himself to the public — for whom, at the same time, he implicitly expressed utter contempt. He was talking to himself rather than to Nora.

The first instalment was to cover the surface details as the public at the time had known them. Today most of those details would have been forgotten by the people who had lived through the war years — or, if remembered, in all probability distorted in memory. And there were millions too young to have heard or understood them. The opening chapters should set the scene, ending with a hint of startling revelations to come.

'It's the motives that are important,' declared Sengall. 'That's what people have got to see. I mean, until you grasp the way we felt about our country — how we wanted it to be great, and stand beside the other great countries against the *real* menace — '

'Wouldn't it be a good idea,' said Nora, 'to tell your own life story and let the other issues emerge from it as we go along?'

'Yes.' He was not listening. 'They've got to be made to see the pattern. It's there today, more strongly than ever, and people have got to be made to look for it. We can't afford to make the same mistake twice. But when you have traitors in charge — men who have betrayed the cause once and will do so again if there's a profit in it for them — '

'When were you born, Mr Sengall?' asked Nora, her pencil poised.

He hooded his eyes for a few seconds, then opened them again and was conscious of her. Gradually, after some false starts, the story began to shape itself.

Philip Sengall had been brought up in the Midlands. There was still a dank echo of it in his voice, along with the other accent he had acquired from years of speaking German. His father had been works manager of a small chemical company which before the First World War had been negotiating with a German combine, edging towards a loose but mutually profitable alliance. Relations had to be broken off in 1914, but soon after the war negotiations were resumed and the alliance was formed. The Hartmann *konzern* reached out also into Holland and Austria, and the loosely knit international group grew in importance during the difficult 1920s. Mr Sengall travelled more and more frequently between England and Germany, often taking his wife and son with him. A more forceful man would have been made a director in due course, but somehow he never became more than a glorified messenger boy. There was something lacking. Philip Sengall did not put this into so many words as he dictated, but when he described his father's work he kept to flat, unevocative details, whereas when he spoke of his mother some life came at last into his voice.

His mother had been German. His father had met her in 1909 while studying production methods in Frankfurt. They were married in England, and Philip was born in 1911. He was their only child.

Mrs Sengall had an unpleasant time during the war years. It could not even be said that her loyalties were divided: she was loyal to her husband, but England as England meant nothing to her, and although she did not loudly proclaim her love of her own country at such a time it was clear that she had not forsaken it. She was regarded with suspicion by their neighbours; and for herself she felt no desire to appease them. She made her household her entire world for those years, hardly ever going out. Her husband escaped war service but worked long hours at the plant and came home tired. She fed him and cared for him — and built her real life round her son.

'She was wonderful,' Sengall said. 'She had blue eyes and hair like . . . like corn.' He brought the phrase out as though he had just coined it. 'She was the strong one but she never allowed herself to show

it. There were times when my father . . . '
He stopped himself. 'But this is not the story of my mother and father. This is the story of why I was faithful to Germany — and that wasn't a personal matter at all, but one of pure conviction.'

'Your mother must have influenced you, though,' Nora protested, looking up from her pad.

'Shall we continue with the dictation, please?'

In spite of his disclaimers his mother was still at his shoulder when he described the adolescent years in which his opinions had been formed. When the war ended she took him to Germany for a holiday — 'back home,' he said automatically, and it was clear that this was how he had been taught to think of it.

'There is no country like it,' he said, 'anywhere in the world.' Nora guessed that he had been to no other country; but there was no need for him to travel elsewhere to convince himself of what he already intuitively knew. Like Hitler, Sengall would have been a great one for intuition.

Now he began to dictate more fluently. 'Precisely' was a word that occurred again and again in his diatribe. But the ideals which fired him were massive and imprecise. Nora became not his stenographer but his audience. She wrote automatically and at the same time listened with growing fascination. This must have been the secret of his hideous persuasiveness as a broadcaster: he was always speaking earnestly to one person rather than addressing a crowd. When she glanced up once and met his intense gaze she felt uncomfortable and was glad to concentrate again on her shorthand pad.

'Versailles was a shameful business,' he said. 'Until the stain of it had been wiped out there could be no peace in Europe. Many honest men in England saw this even at the time and worked to modify the terms. But a lot of them didn't have the influence or the courage to insist. The only nation capable of resisting the Bolshevist threat to the Western world was allowed to crumble under the very eyes of the nations it wished to save. Until the day when, at last, a great man appeared on the scene . . . '

Hitler and his Nazis were true Germans prepared to tackle the chaos of their country and reshape it into something noble. The brutality of which they were accused was not brutality but firmness of purpose. When a body is deformed by sickness the sickness has to be cut out.

'And these men were not altogether alone,' said Sengall. 'There were many outside Germany who saw that this was the only possible means of resisting the danger from the East. I was proud to be one of those who saw. I am still proud of it. I saw Europe in danger, and I wished to associate myself with those who were prepared to face up to this. For a time I was involved with the British Union of Fascists, but they lacked backbone. One soon realized that for England there was no hope of a cure from within: it would have to be imposed from outside. In the rise of National Socialism in Germany I saw that cure. By our folly in fighting Germany in one war we had left the way open for Bolshevism. In Germany itself there might have been Bolshevist rule but for the emergence of the Nazis. It was always my policy, then and afterwards, to advocate friendship with the nation which was in fact our truest friend.'

He paused for breath. There was a clammy film of sweat across his forehead.

Nora felt stifled. It was not a warm morning but she simply had to let some air into the room. She got up and opened the french windows. In the middle of the grass rectangle the sycamore shed its leaves and there was the faint, damp smell of smoky autumn.

'I am not going too fast?' said Sengall with an effort.

'Not at all.'

'Good.' He cradled his bandaged right hand in his left elbow. 'When I found it necessary to leave England and flee to Germany,' he continued, 'I did not slacken in my endeavours to bring the two countries together. There were several occasions when peace might have been honourably achieved without loss of face by either side. My broadcasts were all designed to awaken the people of Britain to the truth. Towards the end of the war

— the second misguided war against the rightful masters of Europe — it was plain that Britain and America, in their misguided alliance with Russia, would win. But any transcript of my broadcasts will show that I did not falter in my convictions. I make no excuses for what I said then. If the war were lost by Germany, Britain would not be victorious, happy, or glorious: she would face a far worse situation than the one she had so disastrously misinterpreted in 1939. All this I said in the closing days of the war; and I have been proved right.'

Nora heard herself saying, as though she agreed with him: 'Yes ... yes, of course. But don't you think we ought to keep the story chronological — keep it to the things that actually happened to you?'

He stared. For a moment she thought he was going to ramble on. Then he nodded curtly. After a brief silence he began to talk again, now more slowly, as though picking his way through debris, reaching back over the years and plucking fragments from the rubble.

'The Fascists,' he said, seeking a point

of reference. 'Yes. Well, I learnt a few things — they taught one some interesting tricks in the barracks in King's Road — but they could have learnt a lot more from me. I also had some dealings with the British National Socialist League, but they were equally ineffectual. I knew William Joyce then, of course — and later. He never seemed to have the makings of a leader. None of them did. If I was to serve the cause and save England I would have to choose other means.'

It was here that his father's business connections in Germany proved valuable. Many were being drawn into the Nazi movement, seeing its great potentialities. Those who did not were soon persuaded. In England, too, there were contacts of the same kind. Philip Sengall's father had for years been a go-between, and now Philip, young and eager, became another, subtler, go-between. Taken into the Hartmann combine as a personnel adviser on the recommendation of a director who was an early member of the Nazi party, he advised on personnel not merely for the growing chemical interests

43

in the United Kingdom but for other, less clearly defined, purposes.

Nora flicked over to a fresh page and paused as Sengall lit his pipe. It was the sort of carved, gnomish pipe you saw in sentimental pictures of plump Germans sitting and smoking and banging beer steins on the table. Sengall puffed happily, for a brief space of time carried back to the happier days when the future had seemed so magnificent.

He said: 'It was at this time that I met a great many influential people in this country. Their names must wait until the second instalment. Your uncle believes that this introductory chapter should tell the story as the rest of the world remembers it — or thinks it remembers it. Then we will go over it again, showing them bit by bit how little they really know.' He paced up and down, pushing his feet down as though to stamp the words into the floor.

War had come in spite of all they had planned. War, with Great Britain and Germany on opposing sides instead of standing shoulder to shoulder against

Bolshevism. Even then all was not lost. The ghastly blunder might still be put right. Even after Britain and France had declared war there was no immediate outbreak of hostilities apart from naval action, which was essential if Germany was not to be foully blockaded as it had been during and after the previous war. Germany was patient on land, hoping that the saner influences at work in Britain would cause the Government to fall. Then there would be a chance of building up mutual defences against Russia.

'Germany was patient,' said Sengall. 'But there is a limit to patience. Sooner or later the matter had to be settled. And when it was decided that the time had come the armies of France and Britain were soon overwhelmed.'

A log sputtered in the fire and rolled over on its side. Sengall looked into the brief gush of flame.

'Even then' — his voice became plaintive, urging reason upon the listener — 'Germany did not at once pursue her advantage. After Dunkirk the conquest of

45

Britain could have been achieved within a few weeks. Yet Hitler stopped. Why? It has never been satisfactorily explained. Military historians and the generals have theorized away, but the truth has never been told. I know why there was that lull. I know what Germany was waiting for — and today I know why it didn't come. The plans were laid . . . but never carried out. We were betrayed — and now that I am free I intend to find out who the traitor was, and unmask him.' He took a deep, shuddering breath and was apparently on the verge of drifting away once more into vagueness and generalization. Then he pulled himself together and went on: 'Because the chance had been lost, I had to make arrangements of my own. There was nothing useful I could do in England. I was not a spy and would never have worked as one. All that counted now was for me to get to Germany. It was not easy. Already there had been an attempt to have me imprisoned under the defence regulations, but it was thwarted by some of the men who . . . who at that time were my friends. Unfortunately I could not rely on these friends to help me leave the country. There had been certain changes in their outlook.' His mouth twisted bitterly. 'It was a difficult journey, via the Channel Islands. But I got there. I got there without the help of those strong men who proved in the end to be weaklings.'

He had been sent by his German associates to Berlin and there had started broadcasting at once. At first he was under the control of William Joyce, the 'Lord Haw-Haw' who gleefully announced bombing and destruction and spoke of the war's swift conclusion. Sengall used what influence he had to get away from Joyce's unit and make his own broadcasts. 'Nothing to do with bombing raids or casualties,' he said. 'I got no pleasure out of the thought of Englishmen being killed. All I wanted to do was persuade the British people that there was still time to set the world to rights.'

Nora remembered a recording she had once heard of his voice in a radio documentary programme. It had been prim and unemotional, yet somehow urgent in its appeal. Heard from a distance, across the years, it had been pitifully inadequate; but at the time it could have been persuasive.

Britain had not been persuaded.

Sengall said: 'Towards the end of the war I was left very much on my own. Some of the men I had to deal with were most undesirable. The good men had been killed. All that was best in Germany was being destroyed — and, with it, all hope for the future of Europe. Right to the end I said this. I said only what I believed, right to the end.'

When the Allies entered Berlin, Sengall had gone. He lived for three years in a village in Bavaria and then was betrayed to the Occupation authorities.

'Betrayed,' he said flatly, 'by one of my wife's relatives.'

'Your wife?' Nora sat back. 'You haven't mentioned her before. You haven't said anything at all in the story about being married.'

'As I have already observed, personal matters have nothing to do with it.'

'But . . . '

Before she could protest further there was a clattering sound from the front of the house. It sounded like breaking glass. It came again and was followed by footsteps hurrying down from the first floor, across the hall to the front door. A strange moan rose and fell like the murmur of a distant crowd.

Sengall tensed. 'Already?'

There was a tap at the door. Wright came in, his lean deferentially inquisitive face set in an expression which implied that although he was dutifully reporting for instructions of some kind he had already decided what was going on and what probably needed doing. Evan Downing allowed the devoted Wright great scope in small routine matters.

He said: 'Sorry to interrupt, Miss Nora, but I thought you would wish to know that certain persons are throwing stones through the front windows.' He was shocked by the outrage yet welcomed the change from the normal run of events.

Nora got to her feet, but Wright made no move to allow her to pass.

'I wouldn't show yourself in there,

49

miss. They might take it as a signal to start — hm — aiming at you. Though of course' — he glanced without favour at Sengall — 'it's not you they're after, miss.'

'But what — '

'I would be inclined to regard it as a demonstration, as it were. They have presumably had information leading them to suppose that this gentleman is staying here, and wish to express their displeasure at his past conduct. They have, if I may say so, chosen a futile and undisciplined way of doing so.'

Wright, one gathered, would have carried out a neat job of assault and battery on Sengall himself rather than on innocent panes of glass.

'It is no spontaneous demonstration,' said Sengall. 'There are some of my old . . . friends . . . behind it. They may have goaded others into throwing the stones, in the hope of mob rule taking over and finishing the job for them. And if it does not work they will come closer. They won't stop at this. They will do anything to keep me from telling of what I know.'

Wright said: 'I think it advisable to get in touch with Mr Downing.'

Evan Downing returned to the house within the half hour. He looked pleased rather than perturbed and had arranged for one of the *Mercury* men to take photographs of the small knot of people on the pavement. Nora wondered what sort of headline was in preparation. It would have to be carefully devised: on the one hand it would have to justify the forthcoming publication of Sengall's memoirs; on the other it must sympathize with anyone who, robbed of a husband or close relation by German action during the war, was still not ready to forgive men like Philip Sengall.

'Right,' said Downing crisply. In the past thirty minutes he had organized everything and had enjoyed doing it. 'Obviously it's unsafe for you to stay here in London. Besides, I don't want my house smashed up even for the sake of a good front-page story. I'm sending you both to Laxham. Out in Suffolk where no one can find you. Micky Murchison's away in the States for another month. I'd already settled with him that I'd spend some time down there doing a bit of duck-shooting on the marshes. I may even do that — and keep an eye on the progress of the work at the same time.'

Nora had an impulse to argue. Already she was weary of Sengall's drab, self-righteous little voice. She had not realized that fanaticism could be so quiet, so unlike the ravings of a political overlord and yet so frightening in its own complacency. She didn't want to be shut away with this creature in the country. Yet she knew she was going to go on doing what her uncle wanted, not so much out of respect or gratitude as out of defiance. She would show him she could stick it out. What was so infuriating was that he knew this. A tight little smile tugged at his lips as he waited for her to speak.

She said: 'When do we leave?'

5

Late that afternoon Wright set off in his employer's Bentley with Sengall tucked away on the floor at the back, covered with a rug until they got well clear of London. As they went slowly and deliberately up Viscount's Gate a car moved away from the kerb. A man standing in the shadow of a tree walked out into the light and went round the corner to the nearest telephone box.

Wright's instructions were to spend as much time as was necessary in London, weaving a complex, nonsensical pattern through the streets, to shake any pursuers off the trail. Then he was to head for Laxham. Nora would take a different route in her Mini-Minor.

'Clark will go straight from your grandmother's place,' explained Downing, 'without ever coming into London. Wright and Clark will look after you all right. And Micky's man down there is utterly dependable. The place will be warm and the beds aired by the time you arrive.'

Nora suggested that she also should go in the Bentley or that she should take Sengall in her Mini-Minor. There was no need for the two cars to be used. To her surprise her uncle turned this down. 'You'll go separately,' he said. 'We're taking risks as it is, but that's one risk I'm not going to take.' She was touched by this concern for her safety, so genuine and so unexpected; and then she thought wryly that he was not so deeply concerned as to free her from any involvement whatsoever with Sengall. He still wanted that story.

When she drove the Mini-Minor out of the mews garage into the dusk she spent some time in a shaking-off process of her own. Several times she chose gloomy back streets in order to force any pursuer to show himself. But there was no recognizable car on her tail.

At the end of an hour she headed out of London.

Nora enjoyed driving as a rule but this evening she was too disturbed. She wanted to reach out by some kind of radar or telepathy to check what was happening to the Bentley and its evil passenger. Evil . . . yes, that was the only word for it. Week after week Sengall had wantonly broadcast from an enemy country and preached defeatism to the people among whom he had been brought up. If he had been caught immediately after the war, as Joyce had been, he might well have hanged. In the delay men's tempers had had a chance to cool, and his half-German parentage had been regarded as a mitigating factor. But when all the excuses had been made there could really be no forgiveness for such a man. He had not carried arms for his newly adopted land and had not flung himself into battle, in however wrong a cause; he had simply poured out filth and contempt. And now he would be paid handsomely for dictating several thousand words of self-justification, just so that Evan Downing could get an exclusive feature for one of his papers and cock a snook at Lord Robsart.

There would be no profits for those who had died; no royalties for the men who had been killed by those who believed as Sengall believed.

And he certainly believed. That was what she found so terrifying — that he should still be so convinced, so unrepentant.

The ferns by the roadside were dark, lacy ghosts when Nora reached the open country. Lights glowed in the windows of pink-washed cottages. The feral eyes of oncoming lorries blazed spasmodically from the darkness. When Nora turned off the main road and headed into the shrouded mysteries of Suffolk the moon was high above the trees.

She had a fleeting vision of the Bentley being overtaken and attacked by gangsters with machine-guns, straight out of some early Hollywood film. It would be the most desirable ending. Incongruously she found herself shuddering not at the thought of Sengall's death but at the thought of Uncle Evan's reaction to the damage to his cherished Bentley.

By the time she reached Woodbridge her petrol supply was running low. She pulled in at a service station. As the pump began to operate, a white Aston Martin purred past, going more slowly than was reasonable on this stretch of road. The driver slowed and stopped a hundred yards down the road outside a public house with a spotlit sign. The light bounced back and fell over his head. He had very fair hair.

The fuel hose was lifted from the Mini-Minor's tank and the cap screwed back on. Nora paid the attendant. When she looked again the driver of the Aston Martin had got out and was strolling towards the pub door.

Nora turned her ignition key with absurd care, as though she could somehow start the car without making a sound.

Two motor-bikes roared up behind her as she came out on to the road. Their noise drowned the sound of her acceleration and shielded her as she drove past the pub.

Nora concentrated on the path her headlights were cutting into the night, forcing herself not to look back. Then after five minutes, rushing up the slow surge of a hill towards a flourish of poplars against the sky, she stole a glance into the mirror.

Two eyes were coming along behind,

keeping their distance.

They were not necessarily those of the Aston Martin. And even if they were it did not mean that the Aston Martin was following her.

Nora took a corner too fast and felt her rear wheels twist out towards the lumpy grass verge. She forced herself to slow down. The bobbing lights maintained their steady distance.

She did not have far to go. In another fifteen minutes she could be there.

And she would have led him straight to the door. She would have led him to Sengall.

The thought struck her mind as she approached a crossroads. The names on the fingers of the signpost meant nothing to her. She had no time to choose; she swung to the left.

A hole seemed to open under the nearside front wheel and then clamp shut again. A terrific jolt threw her up so that she banged her head on the roof of the car. The steering wheel struggled under her hands. A dark hedge, set back from the road, spun at an angle across the bonnet and then it was as though someone had kicked the door at her side with a brutal foot.

The car was tilted over at an angle of forty-five degrees. Her right shoulder was throbbing and all her weight was on it against the door.

She lay quite still for a moment, afraid to move. The noise of the impact died away and now there was stillness . . . until the sound of tyres on the road cut into it. The Aston Martin's lights swung in to the roadside above the ditch. The driver got out and edged down towards her, one hand on the side of her car.

Nora forced herself to reach up for the handle of the door above her. Apart from the angry ache in her shoulder nothing seemed to be wrong; nothing was broken. She wanted to be out of this trap, but from this angle it was impossible to push the door upwards and climb out.

The man took hold of the handle from the other side and pulled the door back.

'Are you all right?'

She would have to be cautious with him; and clever. For as long as possible she would be non-committal. Yet this was no occasion for mental calculations. All she wanted was to be out of here.

She said: 'I think I'm all in one piece.'

He reached down and she took his hand. He got a good grip and pulled, while she pushed with her foot against the back of the seat. She scrambled out and he helped her up to the road.

'Thank you.'

Here she could see his face. He was a man of about thirty, with almost flaxen hair and with wide flint-grey eyes. His mouth was set in an expression that might well have been permanent — tight-clenched determination. She was sure she had seen his face before, but so much was blurred — the accident itself hazing over in her mind — that she could not think how, why or where.

He said: 'There's not much we can do for your car tonight. Perhaps I can give you a lift?'

It was the last thing she wanted. 'Perhaps if you could leave word at a garage — get someone to send a truck out . . . or something . . .'

'And leave you trembling here by the roadside?'

'I'm not trembling,' said Nora indignantly.

'You soon will be. No, let's get away from here. No one will steal your car in its present condition. Where were you headed for?'

It was useless to be stubborn. And she was not sure that she could sustain an attitude of non-compliance for long; certainly not for the rest of the night. She wanted to be at Laxham, but she had to make sure that he did not take her to the very doors. She thought fast. Then she said: 'Blythbridge.'

'Don't think I know it. Let's go and look at the map.' He took her arm and guided her towards the Aston Martin. 'Sit down,' he said, 'while I check up.'

Nora found that those few steps across the road were enough to make her legs shake. The delayed shock of the crash seemed to have struck her below the knees.

The man slid in beside her and took a map from the door pocket. It was already folded back to expose the relevant area. His finger traced a wavy route across the sheet. 'Here we are. You're a bit off the track.'

'I thought I was,' said Nora hastily. 'That . . . that's why I tried to turn. But I'd left it too late.'

'You weren't even turning in the right direction.' His voice was dry and disturbingly gentle. 'Now . . . if we turn back and strike off here we should be able to make it in ten minutes or so. And we can report that your car is in the ditch at — let's see — Gibbet Corner. Pretty name.' He was putting the map away when he shot the question at her like the flick of a whip: 'Is there anything in your car you'd like to take with you?'

For a fraction of a second Nora stiffened in panic. But it was all right: there was nothing in the car that concerned Sengall and nothing that would lead anyone to Laxham Hall.

'Only my handbag,' she said, 'and a small case in the back.'

'If you'll let me have your keys I'll lock the car before we leave.'

'On the key ring,' she said, 'in the ignition.'

'Of course.'

He lowered himself back into the ditch and returned after a couple of minutes with the small suitcase and handbag. Nora closed her eyes because the world was unsteady. When she opened them again the car was moving smoothly forward, backing into the right branch of the crossroads, and turning.

The driver said: 'Feeling all right?'

'Thank you, yes. It's very kind of you to give me a lift.'

She saw his severe mouth pucker into what might have been a smile. It was a knowing, disconcerting smile.

Now she was quite positive who he was. She said: 'You're Alan Kershaw.'

The smile was snapped off abruptly, as though he were angered by this recognition. 'What makes you think that?'

'I've seen your picture in the papers.' In her uncle's papers and in others. Usually the same picture: he hated being interviewed or photographed and had managed to elude all but the most persistent cameramen.

'They dramatize everything,' he snapped. 'Damned newspapers — always looking for the trite phrase. Easy sensationalism.'

The harshness in his tone did not accord well with his reputation. One would have expected gentleness from such a man — the man who had set up and struggled with a hospital for sick children in the trouble-ridden heart of Malaya when guerrilla warfare was at its worst; who had slaved on behalf of Hungarian refugees, flown women and children out of the Congo, organized resettlement camps for the stateless and unwanted of Europe, and who seemed to have a presentiment of the coming of strife to any part of the world so that he was there before it started, ready with help and comfort. And when the help had been given he was on his way again. It was rumoured that after each venture of this kind he went off on some single-handed exploring mission, as though finding it physically necessary to be alone for a while. It was said that he had sought a lost civilization up the Amazon, but the story was unauthenticated. It was said that he had ascended the west face of the Drus single-handed, but this, of course, was known to be impossible. The news stories that could have been made from his exploits somehow never developed into full-sized feature articles because reports were contradictory and Alan Kershaw himself never stayed around long enough to be questioned.

It made no sense that such a man should hunt down a fellow human being — unless, perhaps, he regarded it as one of his holy missions to hand over a traitor such as Sengall to ready-made justice.

He said: 'What address in Blythbridge?'

'Just put me off at the garage.' There was bound to be a garage and it must surely be in the main street. It had to be. She prayed that it would be immediately obvious, and her prayer was answered. The golden glow of the petrol pumps was visible several hundred yards away as they slowed into the village.

'There,' she said, as though she had known the place all her life.

The car purred into the forecourt. There was nobody on duty and the office was in darkness.

Nora began to get out.

'I'll wait for you,' said Kershaw.

'Please don't trouble. I . . . I know the people here. I'll settle everything and then walk down the road.' She slammed the door behind her. 'You've been very kind. Thank you again.'

Once more, in the uncertain light, he appeared to be smiling. He lifted his right hand in salute. When he had driven away and the sound of the car had died into the night, Nora rang the bell beside the office door.

She eventually got an answer from a man with silver hair and a slow drawl. She told him where her car was and what had happened to it. He shook his head sadly. She explained that she wanted it brought in and repaired. She was willing to pay extra if the damage could be fixed overnight: she was sure that it could not be too serious. When the garage proprietor looked dubious she adopted the smoothly domineering manner she had acquired while working in public relations. She hated it but found that it all too often worked. It proved effective once more. The man agreed that he would put his son to work on the car when they had towed it in. Nora promised — or threatened — to telephone the following morning. She also asked for a car to take her home now. This, too, was provided.

The son was a taciturn young man still wrapped in a dream from which he had been rudely dragged, or perhaps in the aftermath of some television programme. He made no attempt at even perfunctory conversation.

They drove along the rim of the estuary, a hundred feet above the water. Light seemed to strike upwards through the haze — an opalescent mist, remote from the diesel fumes that clung to the streets only a couple of hours away.

A high wall rushed towards them and ran alongside the road. The moon flickered through interwoven branches. Beyond the wall the massive tower of the church leaned like a reeling ship against the sky.

The car drew up before the elaborate tracery of the tall iron gates. When the bell had been sounded three times Wright came down the drive to open them.

Sengall was waiting fretfully indoors. As soon as Nora came in he said:

'The city would have been safer than this. Much safer.'

6

Laxham House stood so close to the church that it might well have been taken for a huge vicarage. The true vicarage was in fact a small Georgian house a quarter of a mile down the road. It was a pleasant but timid building: unlike the church and Laxham House it did not care to venture too close to the edge of the shallow cliff.

Where the old churchyard began to tip over the slope a windbreak of elms had been planted years ago. Now it formed a ponderous stockade. On the quietest evening the wind was never altogether still. When there was a storm it lashed the trees with a jubilant, unrelenting scream that Nora remembered uneasily from previous visits. Tonight there was only a steady rustle like that of the sea on shingle.

Nora lay awake for a long time that night, twitching from the delayed shock. When at last she fell asleep it was in complete surrender. She did not wake until Clark, a red-faced girl with a nervous smile, brought breakfast in on a tray.

'We thought we'd best let you sleep late, miss,' she said. 'We' was undoubtedly Wright. It was one of the many occasions on which Nora had approved of Wright.

Her room looked out over the terrace to the wall dividing Laxham House grounds from the churchyard. Here, as though courteously to deny any intention of shutting the church out, the wall dipped a good three feet so that from this bedroom window one could see the roof and a corner of the flinty body crouching beneath the fourteenth-century biscuit-and-grey tower. Through the barrier of trees beyond came the glint of water.

When Nora came downstairs she found

Sengall in the sitting-room. He had evidently been up for a long time. He was staring out of the window across the terrace as though already oppressed by the hostility of the great outdoors. After the constriction of his prison cell this must be too vast, too open, for him. Nora felt this, but felt no sympathy for him. He was a man for whom sympathy was impossible.

'Good morning,' he said impatiently as she crossed the room. He was anxious to continue. She had not told him of the troubles of her journey, and was tempted to do so, just to frighten him. But he was already difficult enough, apprehensive enough; she would do better not to provoke him. Wright had been told all that it was necessary for anyone to know. Wright was not susceptible to panic.

She sat down below the great beam of the fireplace. There were logs on the fire, crackling invigoratingly. She stared for a moment into the flames, then opened her shorthand pad and looked up at Sengall.

'Your wife,' she prompted him. 'We were talking about your wife when we . . .

when we were interrupted.'

'My private life is of no interest. I do not wish to have to say that again.'

'But it is. Readers will want to know — '

'I wish the readers to know only what concerns them. My wife is no part of it. She ceased to be my wife long before the end. She was a traitor to her own country.'

The point of Nora's pencil rested lightly on her pad. Cautiously she said: 'Was she German?'

'Yes.'

Of course there could never have been any question of his marrying anyone but a German. Nora knew that her uncle would want the parallel played up: the father marrying a German girl, the son worshipping his mother and inevitably marrying a German girl.

'Was . . . was she like your mother?' she ventured.

'No.' Sengall spat the word out. 'She was treacherous and perverse. When we came to live in England she declared that she would work with me and stand by me

71

— but she was a liar. A liar and a cheat. She listened to ignorant people and began to tell me that the Nazis were evil. In the end I had to tell her to go. She would not promise me her loyalty so she had to go. She went back to Germany, and there she worked with traitors and saboteurs against the Nazis.'

'This was before the war?'

'Before the war,' Sengall grimly agreed. 'By the time war came there were few troublemakers at large.'

There was cold satisfaction in his voice. In spite of the heat of the fire beating up against the side of her face, Nora felt a chill. 'You mean that they caught her?'

'She was clumsy. They put her in a camp. She was there when I reached Germany.'

'And you . . . ?' She hardly dared to ask the question.

'They knew she was my wife. When I arrived they asked me what should be done with her. They offered her back to me if I would be responsible for her.'

'And you took her?' Nora could accept only one answer to this. If he denied it then she must walk out of this room and out of this house. The stench of the past was too immediate and too sickening. 'You had her released?'

There was a tap at the door and Wright came in. For a moment she had a wild idea that he was going to report crowds of country bumpkins throwing stones through the windows. His first words were such an echo of his apology of yesterday that the illusion lingered.

'Sorry to interrupt, Miss Nora, but I thought you would wish to know' — and then the tune changed — 'that your car is here.'

'Here?'

'A man has just driven it in from Blythbridge garage.'

She had meant to telephone first thing this morning but had forgotten. 'But . . . I didn't ask them . . . '

'I gathered,' said Wright reprovingly, 'that you did in fact telephone this morning to stress the urgency of the job. In view of the driver's emphasis on this point I allowed him through the gates and up to the front door.'

Nora looked at Sengall. He was very small and very still. She got up and went out. Wright accompanied her protectively across the hall and stood beside her as he opened the front door. Sengall crept up behind as though unable, in the face of a threat, to run away from it.

The Mini-Minor stood on the gravel. Leaning against it, appraising the façade of the house, was Alan Kershaw.

He said: 'Good morning, Miss Downing.' There was no pretence of not knowing her identity, though he had said nothing about it the previous night.

'What are you doing here?'

He patted the car. 'I telephoned the garage this morning and told them on your behalf that the job simply must be finished within an hour. I also told them that you would send a man to fetch it away and that he would have the log book to prove his bona fides.'

'But you hadn't got — '

'I took the liberty of helping myself to it last night,' said Kershaw, 'when I fetched your handbag.'

Wright began majestically and purposefully to descend the steps.

'Knowing your uncle's connections,'
said Kershaw, 'I had little difficulty in
guessing that Laxham Hall was your
likeliest destination.'

Nora said: 'What business have you to
force your way in . . . ?'

Kershaw was looking past her, as
though identifying the reason for his
being here. She half turned. Sengall was
coming out into the morning sunshine.

'I suppose you're one of *them*,' said
Sengall bleakly.

Alan Kershaw gave him a dour smile.
Then he said: 'Good morning . . . father.'

7

They drank coffee before the glowing fire.
Sengall and the young man who called
himself Kershaw were like two dogs,
ready to spring but each waiting for the
other to offer the necessary provocation.
A single growl or the lift of an eyebrow
would be enough.

Nora broke the silence. 'You didn't mention a son, either,' she accused Sengall.

'It is irrelevant. He is irrelevant.'

'Were you ashamed of him, or something?'

'Ashamed?' said Alan Kershaw quietly. 'Isn't it more likely that I should be the one with reason for shame? To carry the name of a traitor around — '

'You don't seem to have carried it for long,' said his father.

'I changed it as soon as I could. I got well away from places where I was known or might have been identified as a traitor's son.'

'I sometimes wondered what had happened to you.'

Nora studied him incredulously. 'Your own son . . . and you only wondered about him *sometimes*? When you were dictating your story to me you didn't even think he or your wife were worth mentioning?'

'He was his mother's son,' said Sengall, 'in every way.'

'But she didn't take him to Germany with her?'

'She thought it would be too dangerous.' Kershaw was staring into the past, hearing the past all about him. 'I remember how she cried at leaving me, and I couldn't understand why she had to go. I was left with my grandparents and I didn't know why. She wasn't going to risk my life as well as her own — wasn't going to deliver me to Nazi education, either — but I didn't know that and I didn't understand why I couldn't go with her.' He was reciting the bare facts, unemotionally, repudiating pity. 'Later I fitted the pieces together and I knew what must have been behind it all.' He looked intently at his father. 'What happened to her?'

Nora held her breath. Sengall must speak, must show that somewhere inside himself there was a streak of human emotion.

He said: 'She died.'

'I know she died. How?'

'A great many people died during the war. She . . . She was one of them. It's over. There is nothing to say.'

'There is plenty still to say.' Kershaw's

77

voice was calm and level, but Nora saw that his hands were clenched and the knuckles white. 'If you won't tell me how she died I will tell you. And you, Miss Downing. You and your uncle, so ready to give my father a great deal of money as recompense for his memoirs — to dress his story up so that he doubtless appears as just another sad sufferer. The reformed prostitute, the thief who confesses and promises to go straight, the Nazi enthusiast who now acknowledges the error of his ways: all good stuff, mm?'

'I do not acknowledge the error of my ways,' said Sengall. 'I stand by what I said and did.'

'Do you? Do you indeed?' Kershaw was still quiet, still under control. 'You stand by your behaviour to my mother?'

'She insisted on signing her own death warrant.'

'This man,' said Kershaw to Nora, 'offered my mother an ultimatum. I know about it. The news came to us after the war. It took a long time, but I don't think the details have been blurred or falsified. This man demanded that she admit her mistakes and then he would take her under his protection. She refused. So she was transferred to another camp — a very different one, a camp such as she had never dreamt existed — and in a short time she was dead. Mercifully dead.'

'All I asked' — Sengall let out a shrill little sigh between his teeth — 'was that she should *admit* her mistakes. It wasn't a lot to ask.'

'You let them kill her?' said Nora. 'You couldn't have stopped them?'

'I saw no reason to stop them. We were at war. She had betrayed all that her husband and her country stood for. What happened to her was what she had invited. It was justice.'

'What about mercy?'

'I know what justice is,' said Sengall, 'but I do not understand mercy. The world cannot be run on vague concepts such as mercy.'

The pencil slipped through Nora's fingers and fell to the floor. She left it where it was. She felt that if she bent down to pick it up she would be sick.

Kershaw said: 'Satisfied, Miss Down-ing? Proud of your exclusive scoop?'

His father put down his coffee-cup. 'You haven't come here simply to talk about the past,' he said. 'Why have you tracked me down like this? How much are you being paid to kill me?'

Surprise melted the iciness of Ker-shaw's cold grey eyes. 'Nobody's paying me anything,' he said. 'I'm not a hired assassin.'

'What are you, then?' Nora dared to ask. 'What do you want here?'

'I want money.'

Sengall uttered a sound so remote from laughter that it could have expressed hatred as readily as amusement. 'You've come to the wrong place,' he said.

'I am sure you were well looked after by your Nazi friends,' said his son. 'And by some of your old associates in this country.'

'Unfortunately, no.'

'The payment offered to you for your enthralling life story must be reasonably high.'

Sengall said: 'I owe you nothing. I

intend to give you nothing.'

'It's not for myself,' said Kershaw.

'For one of your charities, then?' Sengall nodded complacently. 'Oh, yes, I've come across the name of Alan Kershaw. I read a great many newspapers and journals while I was in prison, you know. In many ways I think I was able to view the world more objectively and rationally from prison than most of you outside are able to do. In prison, you know, life has discipline and routine. One's mind works more smoothly. It can be soothing after a long period of turbulence. More people ought to spend more time in prison, you know.'

'Your masters taught you well — even to embrace imprisonment with German ecstasy.'

'Don't sneer.' Anger blazed up again within the frail little man. 'Who are you — who is any Englishman — to sneer? Even when the English were fighting the Germans and their ideals they were at the same time embracing them. You' — he pointed at Nora as though she represented the entire nation — 'hated the

Germans because they bombed civilians, and you declared such brutality must be stopped. How did you stop it? By bombing and burning more civilians than the Germans had ever managed to — and not as a side issue of some tactical air raid, but wantonly and deliberately and joyfully. You were repelled by the idea of militaristic nations who conscripted adolescents into the armed forces; and it was one of the first things you yourselves did. Free speech . . . what freedom was there for conscientious objectors, beaten up by guards and forbidden by their creed to fight back? All that you claimed to be trying to defeat triumphed in the end — in your own land. Churchill was right to call it an unnecessary war. You were eager to adopt all the ideals for which we stood. We should have been on the same side.'

Alan Kershaw said: 'I asked you for money.'

'To wash out the stain of my guilt?' Sengall sneered.

'All the money in the world couldn't do that. But at least to repair some of the ravages. I'm not asking it as a favour: I want to force it out of you, so that at least when you die you can know you've done some good, however trifling.'

'I am touched by your concern for me.'

'There are still refugees, still displaced persons, still . . .'

'I know, I know.' Sengall laughed. 'I've read about you. And about your good deeds. I never imagined it was my own son. My son! . . . plugging a hole in the dyke with his finger. Of course I understand your motives. You're trying to make up for your wicked father's misdeeds, aren't you? You feel contaminated, and you're perpetually trying to scrub yourself clean.'

The shaft went home. Kershaw flushed.

'Of course that's what it is,' Sengall persevered. 'But it's such a negative attitude, my boy. You're trying to tip the seesaw — and you're nowhere near heavy enough. All the weight is on the other end. You won't change the world: it's not the do-gooders, dashing from one noble project to another, who move and shake the world — it's the men of power who stay where they are . . . and organize.'

'Like spiders at the centre of the web,' said Alan Kershaw.

'Better a spider,' said his father, 'than a fly.'

The door opened and Wright came in. He eyed the three of them with pronounced disapproval.

'A telephone call for you, Miss Nora.'

Nora went out to the extension in the hall. It was her uncle.

'What's this I hear from Wright about some young man forcing his way into the house? You were supposed to be keeping everyone at bay. What the blazes is going on?'

Nora said: 'Sengall's son has arrived.'

There was what she felt might reasonably be described as a pregnant silence. She held the receiver away from her ear, waiting for her uncle's roar.

It came. 'His son? Is this a trick? If this is all a plot to get at him — '

'It may be a plot,' said Nora, 'but Sengall accepts the man as his son.'

There was a pause. Then Downing said: 'Send Wright up to London for me with the car. And while he's away, mind

84

you stay indoors — all of you. I'll come down this evening and talk to Sengall. Have to see how to fit this business of his son into the first instalment. It's all news to me.'

And that, thought Nora, was all too true, always.

'Get the two of them to talk,' he went on.

'They need no encouragement.'

'Take it all down.'

'They won't like that. The son won't, anyway.'

'Then listen. Take mental notes and write it up later. But draw them out. Don't miss anything. This may be quite a story.'

Nora did not disagree with him on this point.

'Tonight, then,' he concluded. 'I'll be down by ten if all goes well. And remember: keep them at it. I know I can trust you to pick out the important bits.'

He rang off. Yes, he could trust her. When he arrived she would tell him that she was sickened by it all and that she could do no more. But until he was here, and could take over, she would do what he asked. He could trust her.

All she wished was that somewhere in this terrible story there would be something edifying, something that offered hope and the promise of daylight and sweet, clear air at the end.

8

Twilight soaked up the brightness from the estuary and slowly stained the fields with long, sombre shadows. The dark woods turned black. From the far side of the estuary the church and Laxham Hall could be distinguished only as squat hummocks behind the windbreak of trees. The evening settled down. At ten o'clock a faint breeze fidgeted in from the sea. At ten past a rowing-boat moved quietly out from the northern bank and headed for the Laxham side.

The man rowing was a local man. He looked uneasy, but not as uneasy as the other two, who were from London. As the oars dipped gently into the water and then lifted with a somnolent pattering sound, the strangers huddled down on the seat. This expanse of sky and water was alien to them. The darkness in which they liked to work was that of side streets and narrow alleys, with street lamps and the clamour of traffic only a few yards away.

'This is a hell of a place,' said the taller of the strangers. His name was Lucan. 'A hell of a place and a hell of a job.'

'Don't know as I 'old with it,' grumbled the oarsman. 'Some jobs is all right, an' I ain't never not carried one out. But this 'un could mean a lot o' trouble.'

'Save your breath for rowing. Let's get there and get it over with.'

'Suppose as you can't get at 'im?'

'We'll get at him,' Lucan promised, 'if we have to stay all night.'

The boat nosed its way towards the shore. The tangled grass ran straight down into the water. They touched with a faint bump. Lucan stepped out on to firm ground. He patted the bulge in his pocket and was confident once more.

'Wait here,' he whispered to the boatman.

'All right, all right. You told me that once.'

Lucan and his companion began to climb the ragged slope. A bird made a drowsy, resentful noise close at hand. The trees leaned over towards them as they scrambled up, and there was a faint wind through the branches.

The smaller man struck his toe against something and cursed. Then he said: 'Hey — see what this is?'

In the pallid glow that lay on the slope a moss-grown slab lay tilted to one side. It was a shattered gravestone. As they climbed they had to make their way round jagged fragments of masonry. The ground had been slipping away for years and some of the heavier Victorian monuments had toppled over the edge. Some pushed out of the earth itself as though struggling back to life.

The two men entered the shadow of the trees. Their shoulders struck against saplings and the raggedness of older trunks. Ivy writhed over the ground and up the trunks like an endlessly tortured snake. It clawed over the headstones and dragged them down, obliterated names, forced coffin-shaped bodystones apart to reveal black hollows within; plucked at the feet of intruders.

Lucan's companion said: 'If we have to try and drag him back through this — '

'We'll do it,' said Lucan, 'if he loses both eyes and his hands on the way.'

They emerged from the crumbling graveyard on to a badly kept path encircling the church. A few more steps brought them to the wall that divided the church from Laxham Hall.

There were more gravestones standing against the wall, but these were in better condition. Four of them stood conveniently below the dip in the wall, over which a lighted window shone from the hall.

'Up on that,' said Lucan, 'and we're over.'

They climbed up on to the wall and let themselves drop on the other side.

The terrace lay twenty yards ahead across the grass. The tall french windows were open and light from inside flowed out over the stone and down the steps to the grass.

The two men moved closer, approaching from an angle.

'One thing you still haven't told us,' said Nora: 'how did you come to be following me?'

'A mere point of detail,' said Alan Kershaw.

'Even as a minor character in the story,' said Nora with heavy irony, 'I like to get the details straight in my own mind.'

Kershaw warmed his glass between his fingers. Nora hoped that Uncle Evan would not object to his friend Murchison's brandy being drunk by the two Sengalls. It had mellowed them and made the evening just tolerable. She looked at her watch. It was time her uncle arrived to take charge.

Kershaw said: 'I don't go out of my way to cultivate newspapermen, but I do happen to know a few of the more civil ones. Probably they are not the most successful members of their profession. When I saw the announcement of the series of true confessions I sounded out a reliable friend. He told me that Old Man Downing was handling it personally. Apparently this Old Man Downing makes his employees' lives hell by handling many things personally. I shuttled to and from the house and the Fleet Street offices, not sure where I was going to pick up the trail. When I found out who you were, Miss Downing, I thought there was a good chance that you would be the one to follow. Your erratic behaviour on that tour you made of Holland Park and points north confirmed this. I followed. And here I am.'

'It is to be hoped,' said Sengall, 'that nobody else followed you, Miss Downing.'

'I'm sure they didn't.'

But she had been so engrossed in Kershaw as her pursuer, Nora thought uneasily, that she would not have noticed if there had been anyone else on her trail. Kershaw had found her. Someone else could find her just as easily — find her, and find Sengall.

Sengall sucked at his monstrously ornamental pipe. It produced a moist, spluttering noise. He tapped it out into an already congested ashtray and then put the pipe in his pocket. Even with the windows open there was a haze of smoke in the air; the smell of it would linger in the curtains for days.

He said: 'I think I could do with a breath of fresh air. I'll just step out on the terrace.'

'No!' The exclamation was wrenched sharply from Nora. 'You can't. You really think it's safe to stroll out into the night, on your own, just like that?'

Kershaw drained his glass and stood up. 'I could do with a few paces up and down, myself. If the two of us go out we ought to be safe, don't you think?'

Before Nora could protest she heard the distant sound of a car. It came closer, the sound rising abruptly and throwing itself against the wall of the house. There was a brief resonance and an immediate silence.

'Uncle Evan,' she said thankfully.

As the two men went out on to the terrace she went to the front door to meet her uncle. He came in with his usual impatient swagger, as though a whole Cabinet were waiting for a momentous decision from him. Without pausing to take off his coat he snapped:

'Where are they?'

'In there.' Before he could go into the room she blocked his way and said: 'Uncle Evan.'

'Mm . . . yes? What is it? Everything going well, eh?'

'I don't want to go on with this,' she said. 'I'd like someone else to take over the job. That man is . . . foul. I can't bear to go on taking down that dreadful story.'

'History isn't all gallant kings and noble causes.'

'It doesn't have to be dirt.'

'When it is, people ought to know about it.'

She stood aside and he went on into the room. 'Damn it, I thought you said — '

'They're out on the terrace.' Nora

hurried past him and went to the windows. 'Mr Sengall . . . '

The curtains drifted silently inwards, lifted by the breeze, then subsided.

'Mr Sengall!'

Evan Downing took her by the shoulder as though to hurl her aside. 'What do you mean by letting them out of the house? God knows what they might be up to between them — or what anyone else might be up to.' He raised his voice in a musical bellow. 'Sengall — where the devil are you?'

There was no reply.

Wright came into the room behind them. Downing swung towards him. 'Get some torches. Quickly.'

Wright moved fast. Within the minute they were descending the terrace steps. The beams of the torches slashed through the darkness.

They did not have far to go. A few yards from the terrace Alan Kershaw lay face down in the grass. When Wright bent over him he moaned and stirred painfully.

There was no sign of Philip Sengall.

2

Traitor's Shadow

1

They met on Sunday afternoon in Robsart's flat. Robsart had decided to stay the weekend in town so that he could get a copy of Downing's *Sunday Mercury* hot from the press and decide what, if anything, to do about it. Braithwaite came up to London by an early train and Tenby drove in from his home outside Cambridge. They arrived within two minutes of each other.

Tenby's expression was grave and statesmanlike. Robsart wondered if he had practised it before a mirror and then kept it in place all the way from Cambridge; it might have been specifically assumed in order to irritate Henstock when he arrived.

Braithwaite said: 'Not sure we need this

council of war, after all. The first instalment's not too terrible. Dosn't give anything important away.'

'It threatens a lot in the second instalment,' Robsart pointed out.

'If there *is* a second. Depends on what all this adds up to.'

Braithwaite tapped the crumpled front page of his copy of the *Sunday Mercury*, folded and re-folded during his train journey. The centre column with the banner headline told of Philip Sengall's disappearance. The story referred to certain elements in the country who would be glad to silence Sengall. It did not say how much Sengall had divulged before he was whisked away.

Tenby said: 'Is this Henstock's doing?'

'I believe he had a lead,' said Robsart. 'When I spoke to him he said he hoped to have news for us when he got here. Until he arrives I can tell you nothing.' He indicated the tray on the long teak table. 'Coffee?'

'Thank you,' said Tenby.

'Not for me,' said Braithwaite. He chose a chair that bulged as plumply as himself, and settled into it. 'Had a pot of tea on the train with my bacon and eggs.'

Braithwaite came from Lancashire. He smoked a pipe, not because he enjoyed it but because it gave him an air of bluff reliability. He laughed at the end of most of his sentences. His accent was blurred by years of work in London and abroad, but like most shrewd men from the North he exaggerated it in times of stress. The years had taught him that there was nothing like blunt naïvety when it came to undermining more subtle, more powerful people than himself.

Robsart said: 'We don't want to discuss the situation before Henstock arrives. What he has to say may make many of our speculations invalid.'

There was a protracted silence. Braithwaite picked up his newspaper again and glowered at it. Tenby walked slowly about the room with his coffee-cup and saucer in one hand. He studied Robsart's pictures, which he had seen often enough before, with a lack of response which could have been insulting. Yet when his gaze crossed his host's, there was a gentle glow of complicity in his eyes, as though he accepted Robsart and shut Braithwaite out.

'I've been reading your memoirs,' Robsart found himself saying, almost respectfully.

'Another review copy, doubtless? How can an author make a penny when so many copies are scattered to the unheeding winds?'

'I shall heed,' Robsart promised. 'We may make a feature article out of the book.'

'Gutting it,' said Tenby with a sigh, 'so that no one then will need to buy a copy of the book itself.'

Braithwaite said: 'Everyone seems to be writing memoirs nowadays.' He crackled his newspaper at them. 'Sengall and you. Funny, isn't it?'

'Not very,' said Tenby.

'Ah don't think ah like it,' said Braithwaite, suddenly broad and bewildered. 'All this business of writing life stories and so on. Anything you've got to say about your own career affects us all, doesn't it? I mean, you'll be giving things away that put people on the track, like.'

'Tenby has covered his tracks — our tracks — very well,' said Robsart.

He doubted whether a man like Braithwaite could ever appreciate just how much skill had gone into the making of Tenby's book. It deserved to be a success. It would stand an even greater chance of success, he thought sardonically, if Tenby had told the whole truth. As it was, he had managed to give an extraordinarily detailed and provocative account of his political career, apparently filling in every cranny and covering every activity, without once hinting at the plans that had occupied them all for so long during those crucial years. One felt that if a policeman had ever asked Tenby for an alibi for any date and time since his adolescence he would have been able to trot out an incontrovertible story. Awkward gaps were smoothly and convincingly filled in. The chapter in his book telling of the events leading up to the declaration of war in 1939 was excitingly packed with incident. The reader could see Tenby hurrying to and fro at the behest of his superiors; could see him at home, a devoted family man; could wonder how he managed to do so much in so short a time. And nobody would have suspected that this was only half the story — that he was simultaneously working even more assiduously on plans that had then seemed so much more relevant. Meticulous planning is essential if you intend to take over a country in the space of a few days. Civil war and the overthrow of a government have to be managed perfectly in every minor detail.

'Tenby,' said Robsart aloud, tugging his mind back to the book and what was in it rather than what was not in it, 'you really have a remarkable memory for detail.'

'Not at all,' said Tenby with frosty modesty. 'It's just that I tend to be a hoarder. My wife often jokes about it. She calls me a typical politician — all paperwork, always referring back, begging leave to defer answers until I've had time to rummage through the junk in the attic.'

'Can't even bring yourself to tear up an old bus-ticket?' said Braithwaite jovially.

Tenby's smile made it clear that his

100

wife was permitted to make jokes but that others on the same subject were not welcome.

Braithwaite was not to be deterred. He blundered on with surefooted awkwardness. 'We ought to have considered you as head of the secret police rather than as our political representative.'

'There wouldn't have been any secret police.'

'You think Henstock's private army would have been enough to keep order?'

'Henstock . . . ' The name was a sure irritant.

They were speaking of an old dream that would now never be real, but would never be forgotten. There was a sweet-sour aftertaste. The sour memories were strongest. This old quarrel was one which would never die. Tenby and Henstock had always bristled at each other. If the group had, in the end, achieved its aims, there would have been an internal struggle for power.

A car drew up outside. A few moments later Henstock was shown in.

'My dear Henstock' — Robsart moved

slowly across the room while Henstock advanced briskly — 'here you are at last.'

'What do you mean, at last?'

'We've been passing the time discussing Tenby's memoirs.'

'Too bloody many people writing their memoirs,' growled Henstock.

Tenby smiled tolerantly. 'Why don't you join us? Every other general seems to be having a go nowadays.'

'If I'm anything at all,' said Henstock, 'I'm a man of action rather than words. While the rest of you sit about scribbling and fiddling I'm taking steps to deal with our precious friend Sengall.'

'Ah.' Braithwaite raised the newspaper. 'So you *were* behind this.'

'Who else? None of you, that's certain. You didn't suppose old Frodsham had woken up from his trance, did you?'

Robsart said soothingly: 'We were sure you'd have good news for us. Well, now — where is he?'

'I don't know.'

Tenby permitted himself a calculated, insidious sigh. 'You don't know? Oh my God! Mislaid en route?'

'I'm waiting to hear,' snapped Henstock. 'My men knew where to go and they knew what to do. You can see even from Downing's own rag that they got him.'

'But you have no idea what they did with him?'

'I'm late,' said Henstock, 'because I was hanging on waiting for news. They should have reported before now. I've been trying to contact my men since yesterday. One of them ought to have telephoned. I'll give them hell when I do hear from them. But at any rate they got him: that seems clear enough.'

'Alive,' said Robsart apprehensively, 'or dead?'

'Scared?' grinned Henstock.

'We don't want to be mixed up in . . . ah . . . murder.'

'I told them I wanted him alive. We want to know how much he blabbed. And once I've got my hands on him I'll find out. It'll come out as easily as running a tape-recording. And then we can decide what to do. We can force him to make a retraction, if that's what is needed. We might even get him to say that Downing imprisoned him against his will.'

'You have a lurid imagination,' said Tenby. 'I really do think you ought to do some writing yourself — preferably fiction.'

Robsart said: 'Gentlemen . . . I suggested our meeting this afternoon because of the urgent need for a plan of action if this Sunday's instalment is to be followed up by more dangerous revelations. There is nothing to be too alarmed about in today's chapter, but Sengall threatens some juicy morsels next week.'

'If you ask me,' said Braithwaite, 'he'd written the next bits before Henstock's men got at him.'

'And if he hadn't,' Tenby took him up, 'he may be doing so now — assuming he got away from Henstock's henchmen.'

'No reason to assume that,' barked Henstock.

'No reason not to, until we hear otherwise.'

'I think,' Robsart persevered, 'we should try to work out in advance all the possibilities. In my view we must be prepared for him to tell the whole story about our pre-war organization and the way it tied up with Berlin. Suppose he explains our aims and the positions we were to have taken up once the country was in our hands — and suppose he gives our names?'

'We sue,' said Braithwaite.

'Can we afford to?'

'We can't afford not to.'

'This is the crux of the matter,' said Robsart. 'Downing will have his best men on the job. He knows precisely how far he can go without involving his paper in a libel action. But on this occasion he may deliberately invite an action, guessing that what comes out during the course of the trial will ruin us. He's never approved of our views. And if there was a chance of wrecking me, and then making a take-over bid for my papers, he'd be overjoyed.'

'Ruin us?' said Henstock. 'Can we be sure? Even if we are shown as favouring alliance with Germany and planning a surrender in 1940, our records since then tell a different story. My own record in fighting the Germans is unbeatable. My career in North Africa and Normandy speaks for itself.'

'It's not the past I'm worrying about,' said Braithwaite: 'it's the present. Sengall knows how to put two and two together. Once he has linked our names in with the pre-war organization, he's liable to point suspicion straight at our present association. I'm telling you, there could be an almighty stink once the public got on to our tie-up with Hartmann — once they realized what was behind Tenby's plan for the new Anglo-German alliance. We've walked carefully for years and we've got to go even more carefully over the last few steps.'

Robsart nodded. 'Just the point I'm trying to emphasize.' He turned to Tenby, who was sitting with his hands on his knees, studiously casual. 'Considering your book of memoirs again . . . What if Sengall comes out, before publication, with the story of what went on behind the scenes? You've covered your tracks admirably; but suppose Sengall uncovers them again? He can tell a parallel tale, recounting dozens of incidents that you don't even mention in your book — and which don't fit in with the persona you have so cleverly built up in those five hundred pages. The reviewers will love it. And when you make your speech in the House about the new Anglo-German alliance you will, as Braithwaite remarks, be bringing the public down on you at once. Even the people who would have been on our side because of the chance of smashing up the Common Market and pushing the French out into the cold won't stand for it if they know about Hartmann and the handing over of military control to the Germans, and the reasons behind it all.'

Tenby put his fingertips together. He might have been concocting a shrewd, sour remark that would be tossed lightly across the House — and taking his time over it.

Braithwaite puffed uneasily. 'Look . . . if next week's instalment is too hot d'you think we ought to hold off for a while? Give the trouble time to settle down, I mean.'

'You mean,' said Robsart, 'not let Tenby speak when Parliament reassembles?'

'That's about the size of it.'

'Too late,' said Tenby.

Of course it was too late. They had gone too far. They could not back-pedal now. It was, thought Robsart, a matter of checking their armour, keeping defensive weapons at the ready, and marching on. A mixed metaphor, he acknowledged, which none of his sub-editors would have passed. He said:

'Tomorrow I propose to sit down and work out an editorial which will anticipate anything that Sengall may reveal in the *Sunday Mercury*. Here and now I think the four of us should put forward every problem we think we are likely to have to face and then devise a way of playing it down. Let's have the answers ready before the questions are asked! For my part I'll attack the *Mercury* on grounds of sensationalism . . . spurious attempt to revive old quarrels . . . giving a convicted traitor space in which to pay off his old grudges . . . that sort of approach. At the same time we must consider the phrasing of Tenby's speech to the House so that we can be sure there aren't any loopholes in it. And Braithwaite — you've been handling negotiations with Müller: you'll have to give us a run-down on the present state of affairs so that we can see where we're likely to be hit. Henstock, it might be an idea to draft a letter to *The Times*, which you can sign — unprejudiced observer stuff, you know. Speaking from the military point of view, with a fine record of battle against the Germans, you nevertheless feel that the time has come to admit the need for German command in the European theatre. We must all forget any spirit of reprisals or revenge. You deplore recent attempts to stir up bad feeling and spread suspicion. Undoubtedly the work of Communists. We have got to weaken Sengall's case in every possible way before it is even stated. I suggest also that we should meet here again next weekend — in the morning — so that we can reach immediate decisions on any dangers resulting from next week's instalment.' He glanced from one to the other. 'Can you manage that?'

'Ah'll come down overnight,' said Braithwaite.

'I shall be in London anyway,' said Tenby. 'It's the following weekend that I have to spend in my constituency. Wrong way round, really. That will be the weekend when the anti-missile demonstrators are out, cluttering up the landscape and marching to one of the U.S. bases over the Suffolk border.'

'Speaking of your part of the world,' said Braithwaite, 'you haven't brought Frodsham into this?'

Robsart said: 'I think we may take it that we are the only four who may be regarded as still active. The others have died or . . . well, Frodsham . . . '

'When I think,' said Braithwaite, 'of how you lot used to sit at his feet! A proper lot of disciples, lapping up all that philosophy and racial stuff. And now you haven't got a good word to say about him.'

'He's past it,' said Henstock. 'That's all there is to say about him.'

'He has retreated into the academic cloisters,' said Robsart more charitably.

'Where old men can die in peace and still go on drawing a fat salary?' chuckled Braithwaite. 'Good luck to him. He always was a dreamer from what I could see.'

'At his best,' said Tenby softly, 'a very practical dreamer. At his best he would have known exactly how to handle Sengall. No blundering thick-ear stuff . . . '

Henstock's lips drew back in the snarl of a vicious, ginger tom cat. 'I was the one who *did* something. All the smooth talk, all the cleverness . . . what does it amount to when you get down to it? Left to you, Sengall would still be roaming about.'

'How do we know he isn't roaming now? You can't tell us where he is. You . . . '

The telephone rang. Robsart lifted the receiver.

His editor said: 'News item that might interest you, sir. Thought you'd want to know. Ties in with that Sengall disappearance story you wanted us to follow up.'

'Go on.'

'It may not fit, but all the indications — '

'Go *on*,' said Robsart.

His editor went on. When he had finished, Robsart replaced the receiver and looked at his guests; especially at Henstock. He said:

'You wanted him alive. It looks as though he's dead.'

Henstock glared at the telephone as though blaming it for the message that had come through it. 'What do you mean?'

'Dead?' said Tenby, apparently satisfied rather than alarmed by the news. 'That does mean trouble, doesn't it? Now all kinds of enquiries will be put in train. It would appear that your men have muffed it, Henstock.'

'Shut up.' Henstock clicked his fingers at Robsart, demanding the rest of the story.

'At lunchtime today,' said Robsart, 'the Suffolk police found a body washed up along the estuary.'

'Muffed it,' Tenby repeated.

2

Nora said: 'Do I have to?'

The police inspector was courteous and apologetic. 'It's just that we want to have positive identification, and I understand you did work with him, miss. There's nobody else can make it as positive as you.'

Nora turned to Alan Kershaw. 'You're his — '

'No,' said Kershaw quickly. 'I hardly knew him. You saw that for yourself.' He took a deep breath. 'But I'll come with you, if you like. If you want someone to lean on.'

The inspector said: 'We've got the car outside, miss. When you're ready.'

When he had tactfully gone out and left them together Nora said to Kershaw: 'I don't want you to lean on. But do come. You'll enjoy it. You always hated your father, and you led his pursuers right here. Deliberately, perhaps? I still don't know.'

'If they followed me, or the two of us,' he said tautly, 'it wasn't my doing.'

'But you're not sorry he's dead. You really ought to come and see him. Or are you afraid?'

The bones in his face seemed to jut out through the pallor. She wanted to hurt him because he was Sengall's son — as stubborn and withdrawn as his father, in his own way, and somehow, for all his celebrated good works, as callous. He had sneered at her work for her uncle and lost no opportunity of slipping in the sour reference to newspaper men . . . and women. She wanted to hit back.

'I'll come,' he said quietly, 'but not to gloat.'

The inspector came in and told them that the car was waiting. They went out and were driven along the ridge towards the east. After ten minutes the road dipped down a long hill to the rustling marshland.

The estuary broadened here, its limits marked in the disturbance by a spit of land which shielded it from the sea. A stubby lighthouse and a huddle of buildings stuck up from the end of the promontory. Here where the car was slowing to a stop a cluster of sailing dinghies and a few yachts were moored close to a pier. The wind kept up a tired whistling in the rigging and somewhere a piece of metal clanked like a cracked dinner bell against woodwork. The brown water lapped against the grass.

The body was under an improvised tarpaulin shelter. The inspector lifted one corner and waited sympathetically for Nora to duck her head and look in. She hesitated. Then Alan Kershaw stepped forward and grasped her arm.

'All right,' he said. 'I'll look, just to make sure.'

She shook him off and ducked inside the shelter.

The man was lying peacefully with his head well back as though he had strained to look at the sky before his eyes closed. His mouth was puffy. In this grey light Nora could mercifully not see whether there was any bloating of the features, but the features themselves were outlined clearly enough for identification.

This man was not Philip Sengall.

3

It took two days to establish the identity of the drowned man. Nora and Evan

Downing were back in Viscount's Gate. The fate of Philip Sengall was now out of Downing's hands. His reporters were keeping the story alive but with no more information than was available to reporters working for rival newspapers. In some ways the rivals were at an advantage: they were at least free to comment on the behaviour of Evan Downing in concealing Sengall from the world for his own ends and yet somehow allowing him to be delivered into the hands of his enemies. Or was there more to it than that? Sengall had disappeared and a man was dead. If the man had been a would-be kidnapper Sengall might have killed him in self-defence. But there might be things of which Press and public as yet knew nothing. A contrived disappearance that had somehow gone wrong . . . a journalistic stunt that had murderously misfired . . .

Downing ate his breakfast that morning surrounded by a billowing heap of newspapers. Himself a great exponent of the skilful avoidance of direct statement and ensuing libel actions, he recognized

116

the expertise of the attacks but was far from approving of them in this case, even aesthetically.

The dead man's name was Lucan. He was a London hoodlum, killed far from his manor. He had had several previous convictions, including two for robbery with violence, but if the police suspected that he made a profitable trade as a hired assassin they had never been able to prove it. His death had resulted from a broken neck. It had been skilfully broken by an expert.

The police wished to interview Philip Sengall, as they felt he might be able to help them in their enquiries.

'Not the only ones,' grunted Downing.

Reading the details of Lucan's death, Nora shudderingly remembered Sengall's remarks about his training in the Fascist 'barracks' in Chelsea. But even if he had taken his captors by surprise and killed one of them, what about the others? There must have been at least one other. Sengall might still be a captive. And if he had escaped, if he were free, why hadn't they heard from him?

They were having breakfast in the small room where she had first taken dictation from Sengall. She wondered if the story would ever be properly rounded off now.

Evan Downing said: 'I wonder what young Kershaw feels about all this.'

They still thought of him as Kershaw rather than as Sengall. He had so clearly repudiated his father that his original name had been sloughed off. He had left a hotel address with them in case he was wanted. Nora could not imagine why they should want him. She had no reason for ever wishing to see him again. When. Sengall showed up, if he ever did, they might have to meet, but that would be simply a matter of formalities. She would be glad when Sengall had been found and the loose ends tidied up so that she could draw a line under the whole business and forget about it.

Next week she would look for a new job. She was restless at home. Her uncle's promise to give her a week or two abroad might not apply now that the Sengall story seemed likely to remain incomplete. In any case she did not want to ask him.

Perhaps she should move away and find a flat of her own. The need for absolute independence was growing. She did not belong in this world. She did not want to hurt Uncle Evan, but on the other hand she knew that she could not stay with him much longer.

He finished breakfast and got up. 'I'll go down to the office. I want to be on the spot as things come in.'

Nora was sorry for the staff of the paper. When Evan Downing was actually on the premises the editorial tended to get rewritten several times during the course of the day and then altered late at night before going to press. Articles were twisted out of shape and then knocked back together again. Yet Downing would assure the world with utter sincerity that he never interfered with the editorial policy of his paper. There was something about the newspaper world that robbed its inhabitants of the power of self-criticism and of a sense of proportion. Uncle Evan seemed to bring that instability with him into the house. That was one of the reasons why Nora had to leave. You could never see straight or think straight in this atmosphere.

'You'll be all right, won't you?' he said as she kissed him at the door.

'Of course.'

'Nothing's likely to happen now. Nobody's going to burst in — unless,' he said with wild optimism, 'Sengall makes his way here. He may come and seek sanctuary.'

'It's doubtful.'

'Yes.' He was immediately morose. 'Very doubtful. But let me know if anything happens.'

She dutifully promised to fly to the telephone if anything worthy of note happened. Neither of them expected that Sengall would reappear. He had probably — indeed, almost certainly — killed a man and might even have gone into the water after his victim; might turn up days, weeks, or months later, or might have been washed out to sea and would never be seen in a recognizable condition again.

Nora decided that she would sit down and read for an hour or so and then go out for a walk. On a bright morning like this it would be pleasant to stroll towards the swirling traffic of South Kensington, perhaps spend some time in the Victoria and Albert, and then have lunch along there.

The opening paragraphs of the first book she tried were lame and unenticing. The second, by one of her favourite authors, marked either a decline in his talents or a dwindling of her interest in him.

She picked up magazines and put them down again, played a couple of gramophone records, and was getting ready to leave the house when the second post arrived.

Nora flipped through the bills, receipts, and circulars. There was an air letter from America for her uncle and a picture postcard for her from a friend on holiday in Greece. There was also a medium-sized manilla envelope addressed to Evan Downing. The handwriting was lame and straggly, tottering away as though the writer had been unable to keep his hands steady. The postmark was London, with a blurred black number that meant nothing to her.

A man trying to write with his left hand or with a stiff, recently injured right hand might produce that kind of scrawl.

Nora telephoned her uncle's office. He had gone out and would not be back for an hour or so. She left a message that he was to get in touch with her as soon as he returned. Then she put the envelope on the table and stared at it.

It was silly to wait. When Uncle Evan did ring he would want her to tell him at once what was in the envelope. She did not need to wait for his permission.

Nora opened the envelope and took out ten sheets of paper, clipped together. The handwriting was wayward and straggling, but it was legible. Even before she began to read she knew what this was.

Philip Sengall had submitted the second instalment of his memoirs.

4

The story the following Sunday was spread across two pages, accompanied by blown-up photographs of the war. There were pictures of Hitler, of Sengall, of the beach at Dunkirk, and of the Hartmann refinery outside Düsseldorf. In black type under the main headlines was an editorial lead-in to the story itself. It read:

'Philip Sengall, recently released from prison after serving a fifteen-year sentence for treasonous broadcasts from Germany during the war, has disappeared. He had written one instalment of his memoirs when certain elements in this country of supposed free speech decided that it would be safer in their own interests to remove him. He was kidnapped, and a man died during his attempts to escape. The *Sunday Mercury* has from the beginning co-operated with the police in their efforts to find Philip Sengall and to establish the truth about the man's death. But in the meantime we have learnt that Philip Sengall is still alive and in hiding. The second instalment of these frank memoirs has been sent to us from his place of refuge.

'We are printing this material just as it reached us. All the facts tally with verbal discussions Mr Sengall had with our editorial staff before his disappearance and we are convinced of the authenticity of this instalment. And we appeal to Philip Sengall to come forward and trust in the justice of Great Britain. He can explain recent events to the police — and more distant events to the public of this country. The *Sunday Mercury* will continue to offer him every facility for telling the truth.'

The instalment itself did not so much take up where Sengall had left off as develop a parallel theme. It was the theme which Downing had been particularly anxious to see amplified.

Sengall told of a cabal. He wrote about it proudly, without the sad platitudes of excuse that so often creep into newspaper autobiographies. There was no 'had I but known then' and no 'I allowed myself to be misled'. He told what was to him the noble tale of a group of martyrs whose example might yet save the Western world. The fact that some had at the last minute escaped martyrdom and recanted their faith did not alter the basic truths of their original creed.

'It has been said,' the article began, 'that Great Britain was plunged into war with Germany because of the influence of certain wealthy families and certain groups. Only a short time ago a broadcast on Moscow Radio by Maisky, one-time Soviet Ambassador to this country, said that the Cliveden Set and Neville Chamberlain brought disaster to Britain by spurning a Russian alliance and putting forward a deliberately unworkable security plan which would eventually bring Germany and Russia into conflict. When these two had been bled white by bitter war a Pax Britannica would be dictated to Europe.

'Nothing could be a more perverse distortion of the truth. The mere fact that such views are put forward by a leading Communist should open the eyes of those who still think the war against Germany was a righteous one. What better testimony could there be to its folly? Those elements which favoured friendship with Germany had the true interests of this country at heart. While I was still in prison, finishing the sentence imposed on me because of my sincerely held convictions, I read the memoirs of a distinguished English baronet who was honest enough to say that even to this day he cannot hold anything against Hermann Goering, and that Ernest Roehm was magnificent, a great man and a genius. Thus writes a man who *knew* these men. Many others knew the truth but had to remain silent during the war. Only now is it permissible to speak out.

'I want to tell you about a group of men who planned to save England and who failed only because of treachery from within. Somewhere in this country today there lives a man who, more than any other human being, may be said to bear the blame for the years of war, misery, and destruction.

'I am the only member of the group who has remained faithful to its original principles. It was no Cliveden Set. It was an organization of practical men from all walks of life, accustomed to the exercise of power and ready to lead the way to a finer Europe and a finer world. I was one of them and proud to be one. I will tell you about the others.'

He told; but yet without naming names. These were reserved for his third instalment, when he promised to tell what the survivors were doing today. He was playing cat-and-mouse with his readers and with those survivors — just as, thought Nora when she read the manuscript and then read the printed version, he had probably done with his wife. He had that sort of mind.

The cabal had been made up of ten key men. Each had his own function to fulfil when the time came, but all deferred to one man who was not so much a leader as a teacher. He was a scholar and an inspiration to them all. He could make a coherent philosophical whole out of the fragments brought to him by the military, political, and economic experts.

Here Sengall allowed himself one provocative signpost. He admitted that the discussions had taken place largely in and around a Cambridge college. He himself was not a university man. He did not belong to the inner, privileged circle, but because of his connections and because of the respectful remarks that filtered back to the group from their German friends in high places, he found himself being accepted as one of them.

The college was not a pale imitation of All Souls. Indeed, could anything have been paler than All Souls? The part played by that Oxford college had been known to many at the time. It was too pathetic to be taken seriously. Its Fellows and their associates had freely proclaimed their belief in the appeasement of Germany and had equally freely made it clear that they considered themselves men of some consequence. For nearly sixty years *The Times* was edited by one Fellow of All Souls or another, and in those crucial years before the war its then editor used all his influence to swing opinion on to the side of Germany. But he was a bungler, and like his friends had no coherent policy; even if they had been able to formulate one they would have lacked the fibre to carry it out.

The Cambridge cabal decided from the start that power could be attained only by stealth. They would not theorize aloud, not show their hand. They would declare themselves only when they were ready and there was no way of stopping them.

'We had to be ready,' wrote Sengall, 'for one of two eventualities. Either an alliance would be formed between Germany and Great Britain, in which case men capable of dealing with Anglo-German potentialities would be needed, and we would naturally play leading parts in our chosen fields of activity; or there would be a war. In the event of an alliance the Führer promised to use his influence to ensure that his loyal friends in England were given key jobs. In the event of war, Germany would win within a matter of months and there would be an immediate need for clear-headed men able to interpret the peace terms and cooperate constructively with the victor.'

When the end of the war was in sight the cabal would use its voice in the House of Commons. There was an M.P. among their number who would rise and denounce the muddling administration which had led the country to disaster. He would not be alone. Others would inevitably demand the resignation of Chamberlain and his inept followers, and this outcry could be directed judiciously into the right channels.

At the same time a mob would be gathering outside the House. Troops would be moved in by the Army representative on the cabal — a general who had known for years that German panzer techniques would win any battle fought on European soil and who could command the loyalty of junior officers with a similar outlook. These troops would guarantee Members of Parliament a safe passage through the crowds and would keep demonstrations under control. Once out, the Members of Parliament would — for their own sakes — not be allowed back into the House.

A small group of men would occupy Broadcasting House and safeguard it against any fanatic intent on making a 'last-ditch' appeal to the nation.

Sengall would speak. He had made a study of broadcasting and had persuaded his colleagues that this was his métier.

Recalling Sengall's voice as it had

spoken from Germany, readers of these newspaper memoirs would agree that it had been hideously persuasive.

The group also included a newspaper proprietor, an industrialist with a master plan of the siting and capacity of British factories, a police chief, and other eminent figures anxious to create and maintain a new order in the land.

There would be hitches, of course. In the chaotic state of London and the entire country after the defeat, no meticulously evolved scheme could be put into action exactly as planned. There would be dissensions among the military and perhaps the threat of civil war. But this could be overcome. Resistance would be unco-ordinated. The cabal had all the resources necessary for speedy manœuvre. Most important of all, they would have the full support of the occupying power.

After the peace treaty had been signed a new era would begin.

For many years it would be impractical to allow the British Parliament to function in its existing form. The United

Kingdom would have a military governor, answerable directly to Hitler. The Royal Family, who were, after all, of German descent, would be allowed to remain provided there was no attempt to use them as a focus for British nationalism.

Working in with the military would be a civilian administration formed of reliable men from the Civil Service. They would not be hard to recruit. Inter-departmental rivalries had always been more important to them than international strife, and the dangling of the right carrot would work wonders.

The M.P. would become Minister for the Interior. A leading industrialist whose organization had strong links with the Hartmann *konzern* would be given the task of completely integrating German and British industry. The newspaper man would be Head of the Department of Information, and Sengall himself would be associated with him as supervisor of broadcasting. Others would cope with transport and economic problems, and although their mentor, watching from Cambridge as his theories came to life before his eyes, asked for no material rewards, he would certainly be persuaded by his pupils to turn his mind to important aspects of educational administration and the indoctrination of the young.

The plans were made. They waited on events.

War came. After the first lull, during which the cabal consolidated its position and kept in constant touch with Berlin so that it would be ready to strike, fighting broke out in earnest. The Germans rolled across Europe and the English struggled away from Dunkirk.

England lay waiting for the death blow. She was capable of no more than a token resistance. Only a crank would have believed that she could rise from her knees and strike back. Yet Hitler waited.

The people of Britain were ready to give in. Defeat shimmered like a heavy dust in the sunlight of those summer weeks. Everyone waited for a purposeful lead towards a not ignoble surrender. And the Führer waited for his allies within the country to carry out their instructions.

'But someone,' wrote Sengall, 'weakened at the last moment. Someone, for reasons of personal gain which I am still unable to assess, decided to wreck our plans.

'I had always been in charge of all records and documents. We committed as little as possible to paper but certain files and plans had to be kept. There was the possibility that one of our key men might die in an accident or a bombing raid, so a coherent outline had to be kept in readiness. Also we had been taught by our German associates the importance of keeping dossiers on individuals. The Gestapo maintained excellent records which could be called on when there was any question of interrogating or reassessing a colleague. I kept the papers; and over a weekend when we were preparing to start operations, the papers were stolen.

'We had originally intended waiting until the German invasion was actually launched before we made a move, but the Führer sent us a last-minute change of instructions. We were to use all the means at our disposal to inculcate a willingness to negotiate while there was still time. The other phases of our plan, including the moving in of troops and the occupation of Broadcasting House, would be carried out in modified form in order not to provoke too violent a reaction. People must be given the feeling that the revolution was of internal origin and was not being forced on them from outside. Only if things got out of hand would the Führer come directly to our assistance.

'I kept all the records locked away in my Marylebone flat over a mews garage. If you didn't know where the safe was you wouldn't find it. But somebody found it — somebody who must have visited the flat often enough to have access to my keys and to be able to take impressions of them. It must have been one of my colleagues: nobody else could have gone so straight to the safe.

'I called a meeting at once. Suspicion was thrown on me. It was suggested that I was playing some double game. There was even a threat to keep me privately imprisoned — my military friend had unpleasant private facilities for this kind of thing — until I disgorged the documents. Among my accusers there must have been some sincere voices. They were as baffled as I was by the whole business. But one at least of them knew I was innocent.

'We argued for hours. Whether the thief was myself or some other, what was the motive for the theft? Would our detailed plans be suddenly revealed to the public? If so, we were lost. Once the main points were published we could not hope to pull off our coup: we would be branded as conspirators and arrested at once; the troops and the people would not rally to us.

'Should we strike now and hope to achieve our ends before the thief made his awkward revelations? The general was anxious to do so. The M.P. was unsure, feeling that too blatant a declaration of our loyalties at that stage would rally forces against us. The industrialist and the newspaper proprietor definitely opposed the idea of a gamble at such a crucial moment. Perhaps their reasons were genuine; or perhaps one at least of them was motivated in whatever he said by guilty knowledge.

'We waited for the revelation that would pull our schemes down in ruin — and at the same time argued over the decisions that ought to be made. And our time was running out. Our M.P. sat in the House and watched the Government fall. He heard the clamour for Winston Churchill.

'To this day I still believe that we could have struck an effective blow. We should have set up our ideals against those of the warmonger Churchill, and the country might still have chosen peace. But there was delay and dissension.

'Two days later each of us received a typed letter. It said that our dossiers were in the hands of a man who would ruin us if we endeavoured to go ahead with our plans. As soon as we made any move towards a seizure of power the facts would be made public. We would be given no time to consolidate our positions because he would have undermined them in advance. 'Give up,' he said. 'Your schemes cannot succeed. Give up before it is too late.'

'A last-minute patriot? A counter-spy who had been in our midst all along? Neither seemed likely. But that it was one of us was certain. And whoever he was, he covered every track; he sent himself a copy of the letter, so that we all had the letter and all felt or pretended horror and indignation, and there was no lead towards the culprit.'

Sengall's writing became confused here. It echoed a confusion that had lingered in his mind over more than twenty years. He was vainly trying to disentangle something which even at the time had been tortuous and incomprehensible.

When he fled the country the suspicions of the others were confirmed. His continuing loyalty to the cause ought to have proved how wrong they were, but the mere act of flight was somehow condemnatory. They must have made swift mental readjustments — perhaps persuaded themselves that Hitler had been using them all along, in some way which they could not fathom, and that they were well out of it. Sengall had run away, therefore Sengall was guilty.

But Sengall knew that his flight proved his innocence. And why should anyone else have stolen those papers; why had any one of them defected at the last moment?

'That,' his article concluded, 'is still the crucial question to me. Why should any of us have faltered? Through cowardice . . . or because of something that the rest could not guess at?

'It was not I who threatened to betray my colleagues, that much I know. Even at my trial I did not reveal who they had been. But now I will speak out. The men I called my friends have flourished. During my years in prison I read many newspapers and magazines. There were gaps in this reading but I was able to watch the progress of certain men in certain directions. They are frank now about the need for Anglo-German friendship. They wish to rearm Germany — because they have commercial interests which will profit from such deals.

They have dug many noble phrases and sentiments up from the past — but is the nobility still there? Economic and military union with Germany have been desirable for more than a century for this country. But these men are doing the right thing for the wrong reason.

'At the moment I am filling in the gaps in my knowledge of recent events by studying books and periodicals. In the course of these investigations I expect to pull the threads together and identify the man who blocked our plans and threatened to denounce us. I do not now believe that he would have been able to denounce us without implicating himself. But at the time the threat was effective. He knew us, and knew that in that climate of fear and uncertainty it would be effective.

'I do not believe that his name will be found among those of my old colleagues who have since died. Attempts have been made on my life since I have come out of prison. These could only be the work of a frightened man — a man, still alive, who has reason to fear that I may come too close to the truth.

'Just as our plans in 1940 were incapable of fulfilment if they were leaked too soon, so it may be that one breath of the truth may upset the machinations of a present-day cartel. A week from now I hope to be in a position to tell you precisely what each one of these men is doing, and why.'

5

Evan Downing made a great many telephone calls and looked satisfied with the result.

'Pretty clear,' he said. 'Plenty of dons busy collecting ardent disciples round them and endeavouring to inspire them with varying philosophies — seems to be a donnish pastime which occupies more of their energies than their lectures ever do.'

'And when the philosophy is Anglo-German friendship?' Nora prompted him.

'Christopher Frodsham, Warden of Benedict's.'

Nora remembered two of her more ardent admirers who had been up at Benedict's, and remembered the name of Frodsham; but little more than the name.

Her uncle said: 'He was a great bibliographer and bibliophile. Still is, for that matter. He's a keeper of the rare books — famous library they've got there. He has contributed quite a few volumes of his own. *Discoveries in the Göttingen University Library*. Good clean fun, eh, girl? *Some Further Additions to Hain-Copinger*. It must be wonderful, Nora' — he grew wistful — 'to be able to devote your life to books and to stow yourself away among them when you get old. None of this strain . . . this wickedness.'

It was Sunday morning, which was perhaps why he brought in a reference to wickedness. Occasionally her Uncle Evan twitched to intimations of a chapel virtuousness he had long ago abandoned. Fortunately he was good at fighting it down. As to the strain of his present life contrasted with the academic calm of a library, he would not have known what to do with a book unless there were some

142

chance of ripping a few bleeding hunks out of it for use in his newspapers.

'This Frodsham doesn't sound a very violent Nazi type,' Nora ventured.

'One of the philosophical type rather than the violent breed. I have come across plenty of them in my time. Such splendid fellows in the theory of altering the world, so long as they are left in peace themselves. You've read Sengall's story — about this inspiring guide, this scholar and teacher.'

'If that's what you call inspiration — '

'Shall we go and see him?'

Nora blinked. 'See him?'

'We've finished breakfast. It's a nice day. A drive to Cambridge would be pleasant. We can have lunch there.'

He seemed, as was so often the case, to knock the wind out of her with the direct punch of his enthusiasm. He was grinning like a boy at the prospect of some mad excursion.

'Why not one of your reporters?' she said slowly.

'A reporter — to do what? There aren't any direct questions we can ask. Not yet.

And I'm not ready to mount a big campaign against the cabal. Not yet.'

'Not yet?' she repeated apprehensively.

'I want to see Frodsham myself. Maybe the picture will come into focus then. I don't think an ordinary reporter will do at this stage, or for some time. At this stage — '

'At this stage,' she said, 'or at any other, you want to meddle, don't you?'

'Come on.'

Nora said: 'I don't think I'll come, thank you.' He had reached the door and swung round, his laugh dying away but the grin still there. He was all set to talk her down. 'I've had enough,' she said. 'I've told you what I think about Sengall and his doings. I . . . I don't want to get mixed up with newspaper campaigns and shorthand jottings and . . . oh, and all the rest of it. That recent dose was quite enough. I'm finished.'

'Finished — before we're even halfway through the story?'

'I'm not interested in stories. I've had enough of sensationalism.'

Evan Downing let out a little whistle.

'You've been listening to your friend Kershaw, haven't you?'

'Certainly not.'

'He feels very antagonistic towards the popular press. I didn't expect you to adopt his line quite so quickly.'

'Alan Kershaw and his half-baked opinions mean nothing to me,' said Nora heatedly. 'If I wanted to come with you, I'd come with you. But I don't.'

'Leaving a job half finished,' said her uncle, speaking on a sigh as he went out of the room.

She knew he was goading her and that the dignified thing to do would be to ignore him. He was only waiting for her to give in. And she wasn't going to give in.

He was turning the Bentley slowly out of the mews as she came out on to the pavement.

'All right. But only because of the ride.'

'Good girl.'

They drove into Cambridge as noon was being proclaimed from tower and spire. A wrong turning gave Downing five minutes of tussling with one-way streets whose permutations would have baffled even one of the city's more distinguished mathematicians. Finally the car emerged into Trinity Street and made its cautious way towards Benedict's.

The college consisted mainly of a long, low building flanking a green and gravel square. A statue of King Edward IV stood on a plinth in the middle of the grass, dubiously contemplating the small fountain which burbled at his feet. There were two gateways, slightly too large to fit happily into the wings of the building in which they were set: they rose up like the entrances to a medieval castle, and it was an anticlimax to walk under their cool shadow and find no drawbridge, no interior fortifications, no grim keep — simply the smooth grass and the rustling fountain.

The Warden's lodging was a stubby little protrusion on one corner of the building, overlooking a meadow known as Benedict's Piece. On the other side of a paved walk was the miniature Palladian building which housed Benedict's famous library. The Warden could get from his own front door to the side entrance of the library without getting more than lightly sprinkled with rain even in the worst weather.

A few golden leaves drifted along the walk as Evan Downing pulled the iron bell handle. Somewhere a choir sang. Nora liked to think that the sound was coming from a college chapel, but it was more probable that somewhere a radio was turned up loud beside an open window.

The door opened. An imposing figure stood in the opening. He was tall and bony, with the ascetic face of a saint who had made the most of life before deciding it was time to go in for a bit of suffering. It was the face of a scholar, a savant, a Benedict's man from eager youth to austere old age. It was, as it happened, the face of Dr Christopher Frodsham's butler, and some sixth sense warned Evan Downing of this just as he was about to utter a respectful greeting.

He said: 'Is Dr Frodsham at home?'

The butler spoke with the magnificence of the Delphic oracle. 'Dr Frodsham cannot be disturbed, sir.'

Nora was tempted to ask if Dr Frodsham was even up yet, but restrained herself. She could imagine just how the man's head would tilt and how his voice would come even more piercingly down his nose.

'We've come quite a long way,' said Downing in his most seductive tone. 'I'd hate to miss him. I don't know when we shall be passing through Cambridge again.'

The butler recognized the note of authority when he heard it — all the more recognizable by its smooth civility.

'May I have your name, sir?'

'Downing. Evan Downing.'

'You are one of Dr. Frodsham's old students?'

Downing flinched. Nora suppressed a gasp of delight. But she had to admire her uncle's speedy recovery. 'No, I'm afraid not. We met at a conference about five years ago. Dr Frodsham will remember my name, I am sure.'

He sounded sure. Nora could not tell whether there had ever been such a conference. She could not tell whether her uncle had in fact on some occasion met Frodsham. And if she couldn't tell it was unlikely that the watchman at the door would be able to see through Evan Downing.

'It's really rather urgent,' Downing added rashly.

'Urgent, sir?'

His incredulity was such that Nora was tempted to invent a story about having ridden post-haste bearing a thousand-year-old manuscript that would crumble into powder ten minutes from now unless Frodsham breathed on it.

'It concerns Dr Frodsham's German studies,' said Downing. 'There are some questions I would like to put to him. I know he will be interested.'

The door was given a tug which opened it another inch. Downing took this as an invitation to enter. He stepped forward. Nora followed. They both went down three inches on to a stone-flagged floor which jarred Nora's spine and threw her against her uncle's back.

'Perhaps you will sit in here, miss . . .

sir. I trust I shall not keep you long.'

They were shown into a small room with mullioned windows. The proportions were as wrong as those of the gateways outside. The room looked aged and baronial, yet was as small as the sitting-room of a semi-detached house. Curtains and furniture coverings were chintzy but did not suggest any feminine presence. The colours were faded, the yellowing walls looked as though they had been impregnated with pale tobacco, and there was an all-pervading smell of damp.

Bookshelves ran beneath the window and up one wall. Books stood upright, upside down and propped at various angles. There were also three heaps of books on the floor. Half-corrected galley proofs lay on the window-ledge. Downing glanced at them automatically with a professional eye. Nora joined him at the window and also looked down.

Erhard Ratdolt von Augsburg und Johann Müller von Königsberg als Drucker astronomischer Bücher.

Frodsham, however old and doddery he might be, was evidently still at it.

Feet shuffled across the passage outside. Frodsham came into the room.

He did not look like an inspirer of men. Nor, thought Nora with a twinge of disappointment, did the litter of books and papers fill one with any confidence in his capabilities as a man who, as Sengall had expressed it, could make a coherent whole out of fragments. She had expected someone more imposing — someone sinister yet impressive.

The yellowed lips opened. The shock of white hair was bright against the jumbled bookshelves. The old man, bending forward, seemed to be seeking for words as though they were individual volumes on the confused shelves.

At last he said: 'Mr — ah — Downing? You want to see me. You *do* want to see me?' Even on this simple matter he appeared to be afflicted by what might have been philosophic doubt.

Downing held out his hand. A finely wrought claw brushed it and fell away.

'My niece, Nora.'

The hand quavered out again.

'It's very good of you to see us,' said

Downing. 'Particularly as you must be very busy.'

'Very busy. Yes. *Particularly* as I am very busy.' Frodsham swilled the concept round his mouth and tried the flavour. 'Do you suppose, Mr . . . er . . . do you suppose certain gestures are more noble if made when one is busy? Or supposed by others to be busy? Or does pressure of work in itself not give one, in fact, greater ability to cope with additional pressure, thereby making it easy and therefore less worthy? It depends, of course, on what we mean by worthy. Now, Burckhardt . . . ah, yes . . .'

He was still standing there but was no longer in the room. He was carrying on a happy internal discussion.

Nora coughed gently.

Frodsham started. 'Miss . . . er . . .' The sight of a girl in his house rendered him suddenly uneasy. He turned to her uncle for solace. 'Mr . . . Downing.'

'I don't think you remember me,' said Downing.

'I had a youngster called Downing here — no, it was Downley. And that was in

'36, and I think you would be rather older than that.'

'I never studied with you, sir. It is my loss.'

'Depends what your subject was,' said Frodsham magnanimously.

'We met,' said Downing, 'in Edinburgh, I think it was.'

'Edinburgh.' Frodsham clutched at the lifeline thankfully. 'I am sure that must have been it. When they had those cameras trained on us.' He snuffled a choked, dusty laugh. 'I cannot imagine what our discussions seemed like to people outside, far away. It was impossible to concentrate when those strange things edged to and fro.'

'Television — '

'There's a lot of it about these days,' said Frodsham. 'I understand some of our younger chaps make frequent appearances. Young Taylor's one, I understand. And a chap called Bullock.'

Downing took up the opportunity with a readiness that Nora had known before but which never failed to evoke her reluctant admiration. Spasmodic, disjointed remarks were transformed into a conversation which could be steered whichever way Downing desired when he desired it.

'Have you ever considered appearing before the cameras, Dr Frodsham?'

Frodsham grew belatedly conscious of his duties as a host. He waved them vaguely towards chairs, and lowered himself stiffly into the most comfortable armchair. He wriggled for a moment, then pushed his long fingers down beside the cushion. They emerged clutching a red spotted handkerchief. Frodsham beamed with triumph and began to pick his right ear with a twist in the handkerchief.

'What would I be expected to do?'

'Your subject is an interesting one — '

'A remarkable understatement.'

'To a lot of people it would be a difficult one to grasp,' said Downing respectfully. 'But I am sure you could make it . . . er . . . interesting.'

'When I was studying the techniques of the earliest German printers,' said Frodsham abruptly, 'especially those who emigrated to Italy . . . '

It was as though he had suddenly decided that this was an audition and that he must burst into song to prove that he was just what the programme planners were looking for. Within a few seconds he was lost in the undergrowth of his tangled knowledge, where one strain fought with another and one scholar's theories proliferated at the expense of a less fortunate pedant. Sometimes he rambled inconclusively between creepers and parasitical growths. Then, jabbed by a thorn into wakefulness, he would plunge forward.

When he stopped there was a long pause. It was impossible to make a suitable response. One could not just nod and say 'Yes' or 'No' or 'That's quite a point'.

Downing carefully felt his way forward. 'I don't know if you have ever considered writing — '

'Writing? I have done little else. Little else.' The old man chuckled with some self-satisfaction. 'What little influence I have had in this materialistic world has been largely exerted through my humble little books. I fear I have added rather a large number of books to the already large store which the world possessed.'

'I was thinking not so much of books as — '

'The library!' cried Frodsham. 'Naturally you will want to see the library.'

They could do little else but agree that they wished to see Benedict's most cherished possession. Frodsham was on his feet at once, wavering towards the door. When Nora and Downing followed they found that the old man moved faster than one would have expected. His library was a magnet, drawing him swiftly towards it.

Nora had anticipated seeing a huge room with two or three landings around the walls, lined from floor to ceiling with books. In point of fact the library was made up of several rooms on two storeys. At one time perhaps they had been orderly and well classified. Or had it always been a scholarly principle that there should be confusion everywhere? Benedict's renowned library was Frodsham's study amplified and extended a hundred times.

'A beautiful old building,' said their host, scuttling ahead and stooping with the acquired skill of a man who knew exactly where his head was likely to meet a low beam. 'My predecessor made some alterations to the fabric, but apart from those minor changes it has been like this for four centuries.' He stumbled over a book and came back to pick it up lovingly. He put it on a shelf close to his right shoulder. Either he had an all-embracing knowledge of the placing of all the volumes in the building or he had ceased to attach any importance to such trivialities. 'Down here!' he cried unexpectedly.

They went down a narrow passage. It had been narrow in the first place. Now that it was lined on both sides with bookshelves it was not a thoroughfare which a plump student could have used.

'We are inside the walls,' explained Frodsham, turning abruptly so that Nora was almost sandwiched between him and her uncle. 'A lot of these corridors are actually built inside the old walls. You could get lost in here. That is' — he shook

157

his mane of silver hair proudly — '*some unfortunates could.*'

He disappeared round a corner. Nora was not sure whether this was planned as a game of hide-and-seek, but after that remark she did not fancy Uncle Evan and herself being left to find their way out of this maze. They hurried on, to find Frodsham waiting for them, evidently in need of an audience.

'Here we have the section devoted to printing history.'

It was a square room with six glass-topped cases in the centre. The planking of the floor was highly polished and creaked with every step one took across it. The only light came from the glass roof. The glass was tinted green and this had a more devastating effect on the room — and on Frodsham — than the most modern street lamps could have had.

Nora shuddered although she was not cold. Whatever inefficiencies there might be in the library itself, the central heating worked well enough. There was none of the expected smell of damp books.

Instead the atmosphere was dry, filled with the dusty emanations of thousands of ancient volumes.

Nora sneezed.

Frodsham said: 'This room is the exact centre of the building. In here there is no sound from the outside world apart from that of the occasional flying machine overhead. We have held many meetings in here. Many important discussions,' he said nostalgically, 'took place here in the past.'

'Including plans for an Anglo-German alliance?' said Downing.

Nora tensed. No sound from the outside world, Frodsham had said. It was true. There was utter stillness. When she shifted her weight from one foot to another there was a loud creak from the floor; then silence again.

If Frodsham heard anything it must have been an echo from the past. Perhaps he was surrounded by remembered voices. He appeared to be listening.

Downing persevered: 'You were the leader of a group, weren't you, Dr Frodsham? They brought their problems to you. It was you who showed how the English way of life should be remodelled on the German pattern — by force if necessary . . . wasn't it?'

Surely, thought Nora, he was hammering it too hard, too soon. She felt prickles of embarrassment. The old man's hooded eyes would suddenly be clear and comprehending, and he would be devastating in his answers.

Frodsham blinked, still peering into a flicker of brightness and darkness, of spinning memories.

'Force?' he said. 'Say, rather, discipline. Yes, discipline. That was what we needed. A scholar needs it, a soldier needs it, a craftsman of any real worth needs it. Why not, then, the ordinary man in his ordinary job and in his everyday life? If the truly intelligent man submits himself to an arduous discipline why should the lesser intellects disrupt the civilized world by eschewing all discipline? It is not the truly great man who babbles about democracy and individual freedom. The great man has his freedom wherever he may be. Every

160

really fine mind understands the beauty of a rigid personal and intellectual pattern of life. And for those who cannot understand, a lead must be given.'

Downing moved in closer as though to hit harder from a closer range. He rested his left hand on the corner of one of the glass-topped cases. He said:

'You feel that it would have been possible to alter the outlook of a whole country; that a small group could have changed the temperaments of millions of people within a matter of months?'

'Basically every man longs for a routine.'

'Imposed on him from without?'

'How else? If he tries to create his own routine he makes allowance for all his own personal weaknesses; and those are the very things for which no allowance should be made. A million individuals working out their own individual routines will remain a million warring individuals, and chaos will be eternally with us.' Frodsham stood in the middle of a room chaotic with books, some on the shelves, some toppling to the floor, and said:

'Discipline. The un-free man — and all save a handful of exceptional beings are un-free — longs for discipline. He is safe when he is told what to do. Every great religion has known this and applied it.'

'But in the end,' said Downing softly, 'Germany lost the war. Do you still think — '

'I know that Europe faces catastrophe,' said Frodsham. 'I am not sure . . . not sure . . . that I care any longer.' He swayed, and all at once the militant blaze died away within him. He was a tired pacifist eagle vaguely puzzled by the mildness that had overcome him in his declining years. Then his eyes came fully open, abruptly, as Nora had been sure they would. He looked straight at Downing and said: 'You . . . you're a newspaperman.'

'As it happens, I am. Not,' said Downing with some concern, 'a reporter. I wouldn't want you to think that.'

'An old friend of mine has been caused a great deal of misery by newspapers. If he dies it will be their fault. He told me . . . ' The eyes were hooded and then opened again. The claw scratched irritably at the air. 'Yes. Downing. Of course. Downing is the name.'

Nora, upset by his gropings and equally upset by the thought of the consequences of this intrusion, looked away. The first thing she saw was a pipe lying on the next glass-topped case. She had seen it before. It was curved and ornamented. It belonged in a German fairy-tale or a German beer-cellar. She burst out:

'Dr Frodsham.'

'Miss Downing.' His manner was a blend of courtesy and suspicion.

'Where is Philip Sengall?'

Her uncle stared. Frodsham took a lurching, menacing step towards her.

Nora said: 'I know whose pipe that is.'

Frodsham reached out as though to snatch the pipe away and hide it, but recognized the futility of this. Instead he turned towards the shelves and stood with his face no more than a foot away from a row of books in splendid leather bindings. Here was solace and safety.

Evan Downing said: 'Dr Frodsham, if

you are harbouring Philip Sengall in this building — '

'It is my belief,' said Frodsham into the shelves, 'that he was badly treated. I remember him as a devoted man. He had the blessing of a mixed parentage and could take the best from both sides.'

'Or the worst.'

'As you say,' Frodsham conceded: 'or the worst.'

Downing said: 'Where is he?'

'I hope he is well. I hope he will be able to shed light on a baffling question which — '

'He's here,' said Nora.

For a moment the old man glanced at her, and his expression was reproachful rather than hostile. Somehow he made her feel ashamed, as though he had forced her to realize that she was too closely bound up with her uncle and her uncle's lust for the chase.

Downing took up her accusation. 'Here,' he said. 'You're hiding Sengall away so that he can write his memoirs in peace, with access to all the books he needs. Is that it?' Excitement throbbed out from him. 'When he's in doubt as to what happened all those years ago, you dig deep down into your own memory and stir it up and wait for something to rise to the surface. Right? Look, Dr Frodsham, any help you can give him will be greatly appreciated — not only by him but by me. By my paper. If there's any way in which we can help — '

'I think you should leave now,' said Frodsham heavily.

'Perhaps we could just have a word with Mr Sengall before we go.'

'Would that do Philip any good?'

'How did he get away?' demanded Downing. 'We know he killed one man. Were there any others? . . . What happened?'

'Do you believe in Philip Sengall?' Frodsham was very sober, very quiet, frightening in his honesty. 'Do you genuinely wish to help him, Mr Downing?'

'Why do you imagine I approached him in the first place? Why . . . ?'

The silence all about them was split by a distant but reverberating sound. It might have been a car back-firing or a plane far above smashing through the sound barrier; but it was neither of these things. It was the sound of a shot. It came from somewhere within this building.

Frodsham turned automatically towards one of the three doors leading out of the room. Then he hesitated. Downing rushed past him. Frodsham let out a strangled, pitiful little cry and went after him. Nora stood where she was, then went into the passage and looked along it. It was lined with books. This entire building was lined with books. Perhaps if all these volumes were taken away the walls would fall down.

She heard a shout, and the pounding of footsteps. Caution told her to stay in the room, that tranquil heart of the building, unchanged over the centuries. But real life was not in the room with the glass cases: it was ahead, along this passage.

Nora took a few paces into the gloom. There was a light some way ahead, but it was chopped into jagged shadows by the broad, awkwardly shaped tomes that stuck out from the shelves on either side.

Then it was almost completely blotted out. Somebody was running towards her. She stopped, and lifted her right arm. It was struck away and a fist wiped viciously across her forehead. As she sagged, her assailant pushed his way past, kicking her ankle and then floundering on into the room beyond.

Through a haze of red pain she heard Frodsham's voice rise in shrill protest. Her uncle was coughing. She stumbled on to meet them, and found Evan Downing doubled up, retching, hugging his stomach.

Suddenly there was light beyond them — a flickering, intermittent light that began to grow brighter.

Downing raised his head. He forced himself towards the brightness and they followed him as he nudged himself from side to side, keeping going by the steadying contact with the bookshelves to the left and right. A sickly smell of burning paraffin blew along the passage. And as the three of them bunched together at the top of a small flight of steps the flames themselves licked up.

They were looking down into a small room set in one of the more massive walls of the old building. In the greedy blaze it was still possible to make out the rich texture of books that, here as elsewhere, lined the walls. The flames were already snatching at some of them. A table in the corner was half devoured. Slumped over the table, his head twisted at an unnatural angle, was Philip Sengall.

Evan Downing took two steps down. Nora leaned to grab his shoulder and hold him back. The heat roared up at them. 'No!' she sobbed in his ear. As the fire swirled into a new pattern, racing like an impulsive child over the floor to another part of the room, she caught a brief glimpse of the overturned paraffin lamp that must have stood on the table.

There were sheets of paper on that same table, curling and blazing, browning round the edges.

It was the papers whose loss was hurting her uncle. The words on those sheets of paper were so vital to him. Sengall was dead. You could see it even through this flame and smoke. Nobody sprawled across a table like that, engulfed in flames, and still lived. But if only Downing could reach those papers they might still tell the story Sengall had been so determined to tell.

Nora heard her uncle's despairing sob. The room was impassable. Already their eyes were dry and harsh. Books took a long time to burn: tightly packed on the shelves, snug in their rich bindings, they would smoulder for days without bursting into flame. But human flesh was more tender and less resistant.

Downing reeled backwards as the room filled suddenly with a great rage of fire. He and Nora stumbled back and turned, ready to find their way out into the open. But Frodsham stood where he was, staring, as horrified as a man seeing his beloved burnt at the stake.

'Dr Frodsham . . . '

Downing tugged at the old man's sleeve and pulled him along the passage.

'Philip . . . the books . . . '

'There's nothing we can do.'

'Get him out. Get them out.'

Between them they forced Frodsham

back to the room and along a corridor where they met the butler, his eyes as wild and stricken as his master's.

'The fire brigade's coming, Doctor. It's on its way.'

'Get them out . . . '

Echoing back from the grey college walls, the approaching bell of the fire engine sounded Philip Sengall's death knell.

3

Provoke the Dust

1

Nora said: 'It doesn't mean anything to you, does it? You don't accept any responsibility at all.'

Her uncle stared down from his window into the resonant gorge of Fleet Street. His hands were in his pockets. His hunched shoulders drove the jacket of his dark brown suit up behind his neck.

'The job's unfinished,' he growled. 'What do we put in the paper next Sunday? If only we could have had that third instalment. If only he'd had time to finish it as he wanted to — '

'As *he* wanted to! It was you who wanted it in the first place . . . you who prodded him towards his death.' Nora crossed the room and stood beside him. She willed him to turn his gaze away from the never-resting street below. 'You're only concerned with your newspaper and scoops. If it hadn't been for you and your greed for grubby revelations in black type he might be alive today.'

'I doubt it.'

'He was a detestable little man, but he didn't deserve to be slaughtered just because you made him talk too much.'

Evan Downing tried to put his arm round her. She evaded his touch. He said:

'They'd have got him, whatever happened. Under no circumstances would they have let him live. I'm positive of that. The best he could do was to say what he had to say and to say it quickly. He just wasn't quick enough, that's all.'

But still, she thought, in his mind it was still only a newspaper scoop — a success or a failure in itself, with no relation to human beings and their lives or deaths.

The buzzer on the desk issued its faint summons. Downing gratefully hurried towards it and flicked the switch.

'There's a Mr Kershaw here asking for you, Mr Downing.'

'Kershaw? Oh, yes. Yes, of course. Ask

him to come up to my office.'

When he had switched off, Nora said indignantly: 'You're not going to drag him into this as well, are you?'

'I'm not dragging him. He has come here of his own accord. Presumably he wants to ask us when we last saw his father and to accept our condolences.'

They waited in an uneasy silence until Kershaw was shown in.

He was ostentatiously not in mourning. He wore a green sports jacket and light brown slacks. His mouth was grim; but that was how she remembered it anyway — tight and uncompromising.

'Mr Kershaw,' said Downing gravely. He held out his hand. 'I'm glad to see you again, though sorry it should be in such sad circumstances.'

Kershaw said: 'What happened yesterday — to my father?'

'You read this morning's *Mercury*?'

'I read them all. Including your rival, the *Courier*.'

'Ah, yes,' said Downing. 'The *Courier*. Very little taste there is there, now. I'm surprised they had so little feeling as to use that editorial today. One would have thought Robsart would have preferred not to draw too much attention to himself. To publish an attack on the sensationalism of one's competitors, to play down the importance of the Sengall memoirs . . . and then on one's own front page to have the story of his death by violence! Robsart's standards seem to be a bit awry.'

'Is there anything else,' said Kershaw, 'that I should know: anything you're holding back?'

'If you mean, is there to be a further instalment of the memoirs,' said Downing, 'the answer is no. Everything was burnt.'

'What were you doing there? What led you to that place at that time?'

'From the second instalment I deduced the identity of the spiritual leader of the cabal. I deduced one or two other things as well, but this seemed the most promising lead. We drove to Cambridge to have an exploratory chat with Frodsham — didn't want to frighten him off with too obvious an attack, you know

— and soon realized that Sengall was in hiding there. It was the logical place. Unfortunately it was *too* logical. Somebody else made the same guess and got there first. Your father was killed and the place set on fire. They still haven't got the fire under control: the shelves keep on smouldering.'

'And the killing — who carried it out?'

'That is something I would dearly love to know.'

'Do you have any ideas?'

Downing indicated a chair. Kershaw sat down but looked as though he would have preferred to pace to and fro. Downing perched on the edge of his desk. Nora, after a moment of indecision, chose to stand by the window and look down at the traffic. It looked normal and safe — safe in its familiarity and inevitability. There had always been red buses going down Fleet Street; there always would be red buses going down Fleet Street. If people got killed in Fleet Street it was by accident, by the dear familiar traffic rather than by assassins.

Downing said: 'I have several ideas.

Naturally we cannot openly accuse anyone of murder without watertight evidence. But we can explore . . . and we can hint. My financial editor and his staff are checking up on companies, directorships, international agreements, and Anglo-European trade links. Behind the straw men, behind the anonymity of certain holding companies, we may find some significant names. And we can sow doubts in the public mind. There is no law against publishing verifiable facts, leaving the reader to draw his own inferences.'

'You already have some names in mind?'

Downing leaned back on his desk and tapped a book that lay on his blotter. It was a copy of *My Country Called Me* by Charles Tenby, M.P. 'Here's one of them. I'm just about to re-read it. This time I shall be looking for clues. I'm sure Tenby's one of them. And Robsart, of course.' He eyed Kershaw with sombre interest in his sunken eyes. 'Why did you come here?'

'To find out what happened. My father

was killed, and naturally — '

'Naturally?' Nora broke in. 'He never meant anything to you. You hated him.'

'That gives the two of you something in common,' observed her uncle.

Alan Kershaw said: 'I just wanted to know . . . to talk to someone who was there. And I wanted to know what you were up to. You hounded him — '

'We hounded him?' said Nora. 'You were the one who chased me in order to get to him . . . to demand money from him for one of your smug schemes . . . and then who walked off when he had disappeared. Because someone had hit you behind the ear. Because you didn't like violence. You'd had enough. You'd very soon had enough, hadn't you?'

The repulsive bleakness of the whole relationship came back to her. Once more she seemed to see Sengall and his son facing one another — enemies, not reaching out one to the other. It was so long since her own father had been alive but there had not been a day when she had not somehow been aware of the loss, the absence. To meet a father again and to find him detestable . . .

Sengall's fault, of course. The treacherous, despicable father. And yet to set against that there was the unforgiving tightness of Alan Kershaw's mouth, the pre-judgement, the contemptuous demand for money. And now the curiosity. The cheap curiosity.

Her uncle said: 'Now that you've talked to us, are you proposing to take matters into your own hands? Are you going to declare yourself — reveal your identity to the public and set out in pursuit of the murderer? Or do you propose to go about it by stealth, taking him by surprise, outwitting us all?'

'How close do you think I could get?' said Kershaw acidly. He flicked the copy of the *Mercury* that lay in its ritual place on Downing's desk. His finger repudiated it and everything in it. 'Even if I wanted to go down into the mire where he belonged, I couldn't get near his friends: friends and murderers. Things in England aren't settled by hand-to-hand fighting out in the open. St George can't even *find* the dragons. They're tucked away — not in caves but in the palaces of power, not so much breathing fire as lulling everyone around them with the most efficient central heating. The real rulers of the land aren't as blatant as they used to be but they're still there, still operating as before. England is ruled from Pall Mall and Bishopsgate and Threadneedle Street, not from the Palace of Westminster. And there's no way of challenging those real rulers because they never show themselves in the open. If I went there looking for a killer, I'd be laughed at . . . thrown out. But in one way and another they're all killers. They've got it all organized — life and death organized to suit themselves.'

Nora laughed. 'Your father told me more or less the same thing. He was in favour of rule by a powerful, secret minority. He belonged to one himself.'

'Doesn't it frighten you?' Kershaw burst out with sudden heat. 'The man may have been right all along. It's a sickening prospect. For all the difference it made to the man in the street, this country might just as well have been overrun by Germany. A hundred years from now they'd all be happy about it. They might even be a damned sight better off, and the world might be permanently at peace. You can't be sure, can you?'

'There's defeatist blood in your veins,' said Nora as meaningly and insultingly as possible.

Evan Downing folded his arms. He appeared to be enjoying himself.

Kershaw said: 'The Communists have been presented with most of Europe on a plate. Germany is stronger than ever before while England is a weakling. England writhed and wriggled over the Common Market, over the United Nations, over German rearmament, over everything — talking big and acting small.'

'And in your heart of hearts,' said Nora with a flash of insight, 'you'd really prefer her to take the lead. You want to be proud of your country.'

'Pride in one's country has done more damage than any other dogma in the history of the world.'

She felt a schoolgirlish desire to harry him, to go after him as one went after one's opponents in a school debate, working off personal antipathies and unexplained resentments under the cover of rational argument. She said:

'Instead of putting your thumb in the dyke with your vague attempts at small-scale charity, why not accept a real challenge?'

'What are you talking about?'

'Find your father's murderer.'

Evan Downing purred ecstatically.

'Find what happened to him in the past,' Nora went on, 'and what led up to the present. Find out about the men who worked with him — and then killed him. He was your father.'

'I don't acknowledge it. I've never admitted it.'

It was time, she thought, that he started admitting some things — for his own sake.

The box on the desk buzzed peremptorily again. Downing flicked a switch, glared at it as though his error in pressing the wrong switch was the fault of the machine rather than himself, and then picked up the speaker attached to the side. He listened, and the darkness in his eyes became darker and yet more brilliant.

'He is? . . . Did he? Yes. Very interesting.'

When he had replaced the tiny speaker he was smiling as though from some personal triumph. He said: 'Another one.'

'Robsart,' said Nora; 'Tenby; and . . . ?'

'Henstock. General Frederick Finch Henstock, D.S.O., Eton and Sandhurst. Played cricket and hockey, as I remember from some of the more fulsome bits about him in various periodicals after the war. A director of two engineering companies and a brewery. And before the war he was on the board of Simeon Synthetics — which, according to my City Page boys, had a strong tie-up with the Hartmann combine. A lot of his money is still sunk in the firm's successor, Cockaigne Plastics.'

'And since there has been violence,' said Kershaw reflectively, 'who more likely than the man whose trade was violence? There was a soldier in the cabal. It could be — '

'It could be,' said Downing with a complacent smile. 'But if you are suggesting that one of our most distinguished wartime commanders murdered your father you will need some proof.'

Kershaw looked white, stern, and remote. 'I'm not looking for proof. It's none of my business.'

'What *is* your business?' Nora goaded him. 'I've read so many memoirs of generals and newspaper correspondents and the rest of them, and they all hint at the same story. They call Henstock a martinet. What they mean is that he was a sadist. He was a born killer: he loved every minute of it. Who more likely to go straight at your father in the most vicious way possible? And you don't care.'

Kershaw got up and held out his hand to Evan Downing. They shook hands in a meaningless convention. Kershaw said:

'I don't think I need to take up any more of your time. I only wanted to know . . . about my father. It doesn't really amount to much, when you think of it.'

Downing slid off the edge of the desk, disappointed by this sudden curtailing of his entertainment. Kershaw nodded to Nora in a way that might just have been accepted as polite, but could without more than a breath have tilted the other way. Then he was gone.

Downing said: 'Really, girl!'

'How can he be so sanctimonious? Brushing it all aside — trotting out the dismissal and saying that he couldn't care less. Means nothing to him.'

'Why does it upset you so?' he said shrewdly.

'It's so . . . so wrong. So abnormal.'

'There aren't many things that you can truthfully call abnormal in this peculiar world,' said her uncle. 'And Alan Kershaw strikes me as being very normal.' He drew the book on his desk towards him, and weighed it in his hand. It was a heavy, dangerous weapon: a grenade that might blow a lot of people sky-high if accurately lobbed. 'Back to work. I'm going to analyse this volume page by page. Frodsham will have nothing on me, girl, by the time I'm through. I won't need computers to work out who did what and when.'

Nora took the hint. Two minutes from now he would be so absorbed that only a news flash about the disintegration of St Paul's Cathedral would awaken him; and even then he would check from his window before getting excited. She went to the door.

'Henstock,' he said dreamily. 'Yes, it could be. Could well be. Henstock . . . '

2

General Frederick Finch Henstock's house in Chiswick was a turreted Victorian building in red and yellow brick set back from a quiet side road and shielded behind a low brick wall and a palisade of trees. The windows were large and there were no other houses close enough to overshadow it, but the trees would allow little sunshine through.

On this November afternoon Henstock sat in the front room overlooking his sombre, sheltered lawn. He had read the newspapers and listened to the radio. He sat and looked not at the lawn but at the wall ahead of him with its photographs of men in uniform and of himself on a polo pony. The room smelt of the past. He felt sustained by the dustiness of the tiger's head on the wall above him and by the sword suspended, shining and vivid, over the fireplace. There had been a time when everything had been easy and straightforward. The bloody ignorant wogs raised their ignorant heads and you sliced them off. Weedy adolescents declared that they wouldn't fight for King and Country, and you made plans to put them where they belonged. Now it wasn't so easy. Direct action was difficult. Raise your voice and they were all waiting to squeal at you. Show yourself on television and they wrote clever-clever articles about you the following day. When you delegated authority, gave orders to men you trusted, they let you down.

He wondered who had killed Philip Sengall.

The doorbell rang. Black trotted along the passage and opened the front door.

There was a murmur of voices and then Black came into the room. He stood to attention as ever; looked as respectful as ever, as a batman of long standing should; but Henstock had relied on Black and known Black for a long time, and he knew that something was causing that tension in the man.

'Who is it, Black?'

The squat little man seemed to thrust himself vainly towards the ceiling as though to show that he was standing more effectively, more loyally at attention. The old scar on his right cheek was dead white with the strain. He said:

'There's a Mr Kershaw here to see you, sir.'

'Kershaw?' The name rang a bell.

'He was there, sir.'

'There?'

'When I went with that Lucan chap you took on, sir. When we went for — '

'All right, Black.' Walls didn't have ears, but there were things best not spoken aloud. Kershaw: it began to fit. He said: 'Wasn't he mentioned in the papers?'

'Mentioned, sir,' said Black with

respectful self-approval, 'as 'aving been knocked out when a certain gentleman was kidnapped. Nobody never *did* say what he was doin' there in the first place.'

'And what,' asked General Henstock, 'is he doing *here*?'

'He didn't tell me, sir. Just said he represented a charitable organization. Do you want me to send him away, sir?'

'No,' said Henstock.

'Didn't think you would, sir. Shall I show him in?'

'Do that, Black. And . . . Black.'

'Sir?'

'If I summon you to hit him I shall expect you to do so effectively. More effectively than when you dealt with Philip Sengall.'

'It was that outsider what mucked it up, sir. If you will engage amateurs — '

'There are no outsiders here today, Black.'

'No, sir.'

'Right. Then show him in.'

Kershaw was a tall, well-made young man. Henstock had to look up at him. He was used to this. It had ceased to worry him — or, rather, he had never been worried in the first place. A lot of great men had been stocky. The tall ones got languid too soon, too thankfully.

Henstock said: 'Mr Kershaw.'

He gripped his visitor's outstretched hand hard. The response was strong and unyielding.

All right. So there was going to be a tussle.

Kershaw said: 'Thank you for seeing me, General.'

'I'm not in the habit of seeing charitable organizers, Mr Kershaw. Or is it charity organizers? I'm not sure, because I don't have a lot to do with such folk. If people write to me I judge their case on its own merits. If they call I send them away. But you're not the usual canvasser, are you, Mr Kershaw?'

'I came,' said the younger man, 'to tell you about my plans for a clinic in Malaysia. An old friend of yours, Field Marshal Whillingham, has been a generous contributor, and your name was mentioned when we talked. I thought that as a military man you would appreciate the value of the direct approach.'

'The frontal assault.' Henstock nodded. He allowed himself time to size up the man. 'Yes,' he said. 'Though there are times when flanking attacks work out better.'

'I always like to go straight at a thing.'

Henstock laughed shortly. 'In that case why aren't you being honest now, Mr Kershaw: why don't you tell me why you are really here?'

His visitor did not flinch. Henstock was prepared to believe that he often got his own way. If the collection of donations was generally an occupation of his, he must have made quite a haul. This was no namby-pamby do-gooder, no glorified flag-seller. But in those strangely intense, level eyes Henstock thought he now detected a flicker of unease. This time Kershaw was dealing with something bigger than he was used to.

'If you want further details of the scheme,' he said now, 'I'll go into them at once. There are many other eminent subscribers — '

'Including Mr Philip Sengall?'

Henstock had never had much patience with wavering and dissimulation. The underhand planning of those pre-war days had never been to his taste and the collapse of the cabal into a panic-stricken rout had enraged him. The blunderings and uncertainties of this last week or two, when he had struggled to get to grips with things, had brought back all the old feelings of frustration — a frustration which had so often been provoked in the past by Sengall and by that self-seeking creeper Tenby. Now, when he knew he should be patient and let Kershaw set the tempo of the skirmish, his patience cracked.

The name of Sengall was home like a blow. Kershaw stiffened as an advancing infantryman might stiffen under the shock of an unexpected counter-attack.

He said: 'Since you mention it — '

'I do mention it. You're the Alan Kershaw who was at Laxham Hall when Sengall disappeared.'

'How do you know that? Were you there too . . . or perhaps' — Kershaw chanced it — 'one of your men?'

'Your name was mentioned in the newspapers. The purpose of your visit to Laxham was not explained.'

'I have just explained it to you.'

'Really, Mr Kershaw? Honestly? You went to see Philip Sengall in the hope of getting a contribution from him?'

'Exactly that.'

'Playing on his guilt feelings, hey? Gouging conscience money out of him?'

'If you care to put it that way.'

'And how did you know he was there?' demanded Henstock. 'I believe he was tucked away in the country because he wanted to be alone. He wanted to work in peace. But you found him. Found him damn' quickly, I'd say. Went straight to him.'

'So did somebody else,' Kershaw parried. 'And that somebody else kidnapped him. And when he escaped, that somebody else went after him again — didn't he, General? He got to Sengall in the end . . . and killed him.'

'What has all this got to do with you?' Henstock was genuinely curious. Then it clicked. 'But of course. You must think

I'm a bigger bloody fool than I look. Is this the best technique Downing can teach his other ranks, hey? You're a reporter.'

'Nothing of the sort.'

'A bloody reporter,' said Henstock. 'That's why you were there — taking down Sengall's memoirs. Somebody had to ghost them and tart them up. That's what you were doing. You're not going to deny it, are you? Sengall couldn't write the stuff himself.'

'He was a fluent speaker and writer — he didn't need a ghost.'

'Fluent he may have been, but with a broken hand — '

'How do you know about his hand?' asked Alan Kershaw very quietly.

Henstock drew himself up sharply. 'It was in the papers.'

'Not in any paper *I* saw. It was never mentioned. It could only have been known to those of us who were there — and to whoever it was who inflicted the wound.'

'Get out,' said Henstock.

'So it was you. Tell me, General — how

did you get on to the trail? What took you to Cambridge? I suppose that was pretty obvious, though.'

Henstock pressed the bell push by the fireplace. He said: 'Go back to your bloody paper. Tell your boss that if any other reporter tries to worm his way into my household under false pretences I'll have him arrested. And if one imputation of any kind against me creeps into that dirty rag of yours I'll sue you. And don't think I wouldn't do it.' His batman came into the room. 'Show this man out before I beat him up with my own hands.' He extended his stubby fingers, with the knots of hair between the joints. 'And don't think I wouldn't be glad to do *that*, as well, Kershaw. Now get out.'

Kershaw said: 'It's not Philip Sengall who's on the run now, is it, General?'

'I told you . . . '

It was a killing rage that choked the words off. It had come over him in the past and he had enjoyed giving way to it. His own men had been terrified of him then — more terrified than they ever were of the enemy. And that was the way it ought to be. That was the way to drive them on: them and himself.

The red haze before his eyes cleared. He saw Black leading the way out of the room, and Kershaw following. Just as well. Henstock held his breath, then released it shudderingly. Just as well. He liked his killings to be properly carried out — that is, in such a way that there could never, in war or peace, be any blame attached to him.

He had to sit down and remain quite still for five minutes. When Black came in after getting rid of the intruder he had to wave him away speechlessly. He got so dizzy nowadays. Anger was only a temporary stimulant: it ebbed away too quickly, leaving him with a pounding heart.

When his strength came back he reached for the telephone and put in calls to Robsart, Tenby, and Braithwaite. To each of them he told the story of the interrogation he had just undergone.

'Downing's on to something,' he said to each of them. 'We don't know how much Sengall told him or how much he managed to get written before he died. But there must have been plenty, or this young Kershaw wouldn't have been round here today. Maybe you'll be next on his list.'

Robsart sounded thunderous, as though preparing to loose the bolts of his wrath at Downing via the *Courier*. Tenby sounded even more affectedly uninterested on the telephone than he did in real life. Braithwaite was scared and made no bones about it. 'But he can't worm anything out of me. You haven't mentioned me by name? He hasn't got any lead on me that you know of? Ah mean, ah don't see what he could expect to find out from me. Are you sure he — '

'He and his boss,' said Henstock, 'want to know who killed Sengall. And so,' he added, 'do I.'

3

'I've got it!' said Evan Downing jubilantly.

He came storming into the house with

Tenby's book under his arm and thrust it at her. It was of no import to him that she might be doing something else, might want to wash the whole Sengall business out of her mind. He had found something and he had to have an audience.

The book was heavy. She rested it on her knee and he fidgeted impatiently while she turned the pages.

'Yes,' she said, caught despite herself in the excitement of recognition. 'It could be.'

'It not only could be. That is what happened. The dates just do not tally. They've been avoided — very cleverly got round — but if you work the whole thing out you can see that he has deliberately blurred his story at that critical phase. It gives the whole game away.'

'But, Uncle Evan' — Nora cast about for some way of shaking his exasperating certainty — 'you can't be absolutely sure of things like that. It's so long since they actually took place. The war blurred everything. People don't remember correctly. It was all such a muddle. There aren't even two books that agree. And

197

those who lived through it surely get things mixed up in their memories.'

'Exactly. We all tend to forget. You only have to read the memoirs of different soldiers and civilians to see that one incident could appear quite differently to each of them. Their memories have adjusted to what they want to believe. No general ever made a mistake. No battle was ever lost. Every strategic retreat was a major victory. But' — he stood beside her and patted the book on her lap affectionately — 'Tenby was unusual. Tenby is noted for his meticulousness. A great hoarder of notes and papers, Tenby. You can tell from his style of writing that he is a precise, fussy man. Tenby's life has more footnotes than text. He keeps his nose clean and surrounds himself with unimpeachable authorities. And when a man like that writes vaguely about a crucial issue in his career, leaving the details blurred and dodging round the dates, you can be sure there's a valid reason. He's like the writer of detective stories who throws suspicion on every man, woman and child in his novel except one. The omission is in itself an indication of guilt.'

Nora could not disagree. She read the key paragraphs over again, and they added up to only that one conclusion.

'And Sengall,' said her uncle fervently, 'with all those years in prison thinking of little else, remembered masses of detail that nobody else would have remembered. Sengall, unlike the rest of us until we were triggered off by what has happened, would be *looking* for just that one clue that would lead him to the cabal's real defector. That's what Tenby was afraid of. That's why Sengall had to be removed.'

Downing ranted on, building up his theory. And Nora saw no weakness in the structure, no way of pulling it down. Facts and theory interlocked too neatly.

During the Governmental reshuffle after Dunkirk, Tenby had been offered a plum job which made up for all the slights and setbacks he had so far suffered in his Parliamentary career. He was to be Secretary of State for Occupied Europe, in a new department dealing with the accumulating problems of overrun countries and their governments in exile. Such a department had to be organized down to the last pen nib before its existence was made known to the House and the public. The offer of the post was made to Tenby two months before the issue of the official announcement. In his memoirs he could not refrain from hinting that he had been in on the whole thing from the start. But by planting that flattering implication he had left himself exposed to the one man who might remember the exact chronology of events in those war-clouded days.

Sengall, probing into the activities of his ex-colleagues, would spot the veiled inconsistencies. For years Henstock and the others had had it fixed in their minds that Sengall had been the one who ratted on them. But Sengall himself, knowing his own innocence, would at last be able to deduce who had really been responsible for the collapse.

Sengall had to be eliminated.

'When Sengall went to hide out with Frodsham he was on Tenby's home ground. Tenby's constituency is not far outside the city. But Tenby had to be careful. He couldn't let the others know how desperate he was to engineer Sengall's death. I'm sure that he never trusted Henstock: antipathetic characters without a doubt. Tenby is a lone wolf. Even in that cabal he looked after himself and no other. And of this I'm sure: if any man in the United Kingdom still has the cabal's papers, it's Tenby. The man's a hoarder. He has built his career brick by fiddling little brick and I don't think he would ever bring himself to throw anything away.'

Nora said: 'So what are you going to do?'

At that moment Wright came in to announce disapprovingly that Mr Kershaw had called to see Mr Downing. Wright made it plain that he would not be reluctant to tell Mr Kershaw that Mr Downing was not at home and would not ever be at home to Mr Kershaw. Wright still associated the said Mr Kershaw with an impudent deceit and some very odd subsequent goings-on at Laxham.

'Send him in,' said Downing.

Clearly he welcomed the prospect of an addition to his audience. Before he could launch into a further exposition, however, Alan Kershaw said:

'I was hoping to see you alone.'

Nora resisted a childish impulse to stick her tongue out in response to his unfriendly glance.

'I've been working things out,' said Downing.

'So have I,' said Kershaw. 'I've been to see General Henstock. Not,' he hastened to add, 'because of your niece's cheap jibes, but because . . . well . . . '

'Well?' Nora challenged him. She felt a pang of an inexplicable yet painful pleasure at the thought that she had succeeded in goading him into action. It was not that she cared twopence what he did; but it was gratifying to think that she could have prodded him in the direction she wanted him to go.

Then he told them the story of a visit to Henstock that temporarily distracted Uncle Evan's attention from his own brilliant deductions. Indeed, halfway through the account Downing crowed his delight. 'Good man! Didn't think you had it in you, boy. I could use someone with initiative like that.' But when the tale of the interview was ended, Downing had grown solemn. His summing-up was: 'Good effort, but you were on the wrong track.' Then it was his turn. He plodded happily over the ground that he had already covered with Nora. Alan Kershaw listened, at first sceptically and then with complete absorption. Downing gave him the book, and Kershaw studied the appropriate paragraphs dutifully. Like an obedient pupil he found nothing with which to quarrel in the exposition.

When the story came to its triumphant conclusion, Kershaw said: 'So what do we do?'

Downing grinned, recognizing the implication of the 'we'. Nora, too, felt the echo of it inside herself. Things had gone too far. She had let herself be drawn in at the beginning and it was too late to struggle free. She had nudged Alan Kershaw off his balance into the middle of it — but in some way she had allowed herself to be dragged down with him.

'Just a minute.' Nora made a last attempt to climb out. 'The cabal was made up of men who believed that Germany would win. Tenby was one of them. If he knew, or thought he knew, that the Nazis were bound to succeed — '

'If he had been out and out convinced,' her uncle took her up, 'presumably he wouldn't have acted as he did. But when he was tempted by the certainty of power in his own country, perhaps he couldn't resist. If he had resisted, the story he tells today would be a different one — if, that is, he had lived to tell it. History is full of ifs. If Stanley Baldwin hadn't done this . . . if the reoccupation of the Rhineland had been stopped . . . if Hitler had been assassinated . . . if the German generals had succeeded in getting rid of him . . . The point is that Tenby *did* desert his friends; he *did* take a gamble. And if the Nazis had won after all, I have no doubt that Tenby would have had an excuse for acting as he did. His arguments would all have been neatly deployed, well documented. And, you know, he would have been able to believe those arguments. The English are good at maintaining two or more separate sets of moral outlooks. Tenby is a true-blue Englishman, filled with the certainty that whatever he does is right because he's the one who's doing it.' Downing was giving way, with a drunkard's mingled shame and exhilaration, to the intoxicating surge of words and phrases. 'All things are possible when you have that assurance which only an English public school and the Anglican Church can give you. Treachery becomes adjustment to altered circumstances; persecution becomes a religious observance; murder becomes the justifiable elimination of evildoers. I am positive that Tenby arranged, with the clearest conscience in the world, for the death of Sengall.'

Alan Kershaw said: 'How was it that the other members of the group were so ready to blame my father? What motive could they have suspected him of having? He had always been the most unflinchingly pro-German of the lot.'

'My own theory is that they thought it

was all deliberate — that they had been made fools of. They were ready, once it was convenient for them to do so, to believe that Sengall had been Hitler's tool and was using them rather than being used by them. They transferred their affections quickly enough and fought for mere survival.'

'But anyone after the war who checked back — '

'Nobody checks back,' said Downing. 'Hardly a person in this country reads yesterday's newspaper except when lighting the fire with it. Certainly not last year's. It takes real determination to dig back through newsprint of twenty years ago. One major newspaper announced in 1939 that there would be no war; and next day war broke out. That paper is still going strong today with a vastly increased circulation. People do not check back. None of us in this business would survive if they did, and a hell of a lot of familiar faces would be missing from the House of Commons.'

'And next week,' Nora mused aloud, 'Tenby speaks in the House on European integration and the new Anglo-German military and economic alliance. Is the country ever going to find out why he is so keen?'

'How do we prove anything?' said Alan Kershaw.

Downing looked pleased by this promise of support, not so much offered as thrust upon him. He said: 'I've already told you that I see Tenby as a hoarder. If you can get at him, you might get your hands on the actual papers. At the very least you might extract some damaging admissions.'

Kershaw did not blink. He did not look alarmed and try to back away behind a shield of reservations and excuses, explaining his failure in advance. He said:

'All right. Where do we start? Where is Tenby right now?'

4

On Saturday it turned resolutely cold. Autumn had slipped finally away beyond recall. Cars parked all night in the streets were sprinkled with leaves and there were heaps of leaves over the wheel rims. On lawns and in the parks the frost was a thin glittering film, thickening to the whiteness of icing sugar when seen from a distance.

In the late morning Nora drove the two of them out of London towards Cambridge. She was driving Alan Kershaw's car, not for any practical reason but because she had said that she wanted to drive it. On the return journey there was to be no argument about it: he would drive. When they came back they would be in a hurry.

Even with the heater on, Nora was glad of her winter coat. The glass of the windscreen and the windows was icy to the touch. The people in the streets were huddled up against the wind, and when the streets had been left behind and the country opened up ahead, the fields and trees looked bleak and hostile.

Alan said: 'Are you sure you can go through with this?'

'Of course. I'm a big girl, and I did take quite a big part in our last school play before I left.'

'If I hadn't muffed things so badly with Henstock I could have tackled the whole thing myself. But he's bound to have passed the word on. Anyway, we can't risk it: I couldn't go straight at it myself.'

'It's all settled,' said Nora. 'We don't have to go over it again.'

She felt strangely calm. The car itself helped: it was so smooth and powerful and yet so docile, so utterly under her control. The decisions had been taken, the plans made, and she had a sense of euphoria that might become dangerous if she allowed herself to float away too readily on it. But she was conscious of no real danger.

'The attacker,' said Alan, as though following up her thoughts, 'has the advantage. The defender doesn't know which direction he's going to be hit from. He may not even know he's going to be hit at all.'

They had lunch in Cambridge and then separated. Nora had a moment of fear when she walked away from Alan. It was in no way connected with the success of their plan. Somehow she took that for granted. It was Alan's determination that frightened her. She had mocked him into his mission of tracking down his father's killer and now he was committed to it heart and soul. This could not be due to affection for his father: it was an abstract idea and all the more frightening because of it. Something ruthless had taken possession of him and would not let go until the mission was accomplished. She began to have a glimmering of his behaviour over the past years — the good things he had done, the schools and hospitals and emergency problems dealt with and then left: he would take a plan and work on it until it had been developed as far as he thought it could go . . . and then, his part of the job accomplished, he would leave.

When Tenby had been demolished Alan Kershaw would move on to his next self-appointed task.

She got on the bus and took a thirty-minute ride to Tenby's home in the heart of his constituency.

It was not the right time of year for a garden party, so the organizers had compromised. An awning was slung between the trees, sagging over a reasonable area of the lawn and also covering the steps which led up to the terrace. The glass doors opening on to the terrace were locked back, and long tables laden with sandwiches were lined up within. As the rain had kept off, most of the guests were sauntering across the lawn and saying that the flower-beds would be wonderful next year and that it was lucky the rain had kept off, wasn't it.

The house had an eighteenth-century symmetry, its sides and window-frames and roof sharp-edged in the cold air. It faced down a slightly tilted lawn to a precise, spiky little hedge. One felt that there ought to be music, if not outside, then somewhere in a large panelled room or even in an opera house attached to the building; but the dresses of the women, when one got close, did not match up to the standard seen at Glyndebourne.

Nora paid her admission fee and kept under the trees which supported the awning. Charles Tenby and his wife were moving graciously to and fro, not so much laying the foundations of his career as, after all this time, ensuring that the fabric was kept in good repair. Nora had never met him and did not suppose he would recognize her, but she preferred to avoid a direct encounter until the moment when it would serve its appointed purpose.

She realized that she was considerably younger than most of the other loyal supporters present. They fell mainly into the category of fleshy or scrawny party workers — women with shrill voices and a talent for organizing or at the very least attending jumble sales. While they walked and talked to their friends they looked constantly over their shoulders in the hope that Mr Tenby would catch them up, or, if he had already spoken to them, that their paths would somehow cross again. Every now and then they would say something spiteful about the Leader of the Opposition or, with even more fervour, about a local councillor who seemed to have odd views on the question of road maintenance.

There were two other young people

who had either strayed in by mistake or arrived with malicious intent. Tenby and a little man who bobbed beside him all the time cast dubious glances at these two. The young man wore a grey sweater and baggy grey trousers; the girl with him had a sweater that was darker than his but not necessarily so because the wool was a different shade, and blue jeans. Both sported nuclear disarmament badges.

Tenby himself, Nora conceded, had an intuitive knowledge of the right way to dress for a function such as this. He was not ostentatiously prosperous; not the London clubman deigning to visit a primitive rural constituency. On the other hand he was not wearing a heavy sports jacket and baggy trousers. He neither smoked a stubby pipe nor looked as though he were pining for a cigar. He wore a dark brown suit and a green woollen tie. He had bathed and shaved somewhere around lunchtime and looked pink, healthy, very capable, and very honest.

An inquisitive middle-aged man tried to make his way round the side of the house. He was deterred by a watchful attendant with a badge in his lapel. Nora observed this. It fitted in with the calculations they had made before leaving London. Guardians of every kind must be flushed out if Alan was to have a clear path to his destination.

Someone began to clap his hands together for attention. Heads turned. Groups coalesced into larger groups. On the crown of the lawn, sloping up under the awning, the podgy little man who had kept so close to Tenby was now waving his arms as though to draw his beloved brethren in closer.

'Ssh!' said three elderly women simultaneously.

The little man let his arms fall to his sides so that he appeared to be standing reverently to attention. He said in a squeaky voice, harsh because he was endeavouring to throw it far away down the lawn:

'We are all delighted to have our Member, the Right Honourable Charles Tenby, with us this afternoon.'

The phraseology struck Nora as being

a trifle odd, since this was Tenby's house and if anybody was with anybody it was surely the people who had paid to come in to this wintry fête rather than . . .

No, she said to herself. Let it go. This was no time for splitting hairs. There was rough, straightforward business ahead.

'Busy as he is at this time,' the staunch sycophant orated, 'he and his charming wife . . . '

The speaker bowed convulsively and heads turned towards the woman in powder blue with the slanting smile. She had a long face, ashen hair, and blunt, widely spaced teeth. The hair was dyed. The teeth were natural: no one would have accepted false teeth of such irregularity.

When Tenby himself spoke, his voice was in complete contrast to that of his cheer-leader. Without effort it carried to the uneven ranks of supporters lower down the lawn.

'Most of the things I have to say will be said in more detail next week in the House. But they will all have to be expressed in rather formal language — for the benefit of the Hansard reporters.' He took the audience into his confidence with his smile. 'Today I feel that I'm talking to friends. And I have a duty to be frank with my friends.'

The wind rustled along the wall and struck a faint booming note from the awning. Across the Fens the cold struck in over the North Sea.

'Since you were good enough to appoint me as your representative in the great councils of this country, I have always felt it incumbent on me to tell you honestly what the policies of the Government are. It is no secret that we are at the moment considering a far-reaching new treaty with Germany. It is a country with which we have much in common. Our own cherished Royal Family is German by descent, our language and culture owe much to Germany, and now that the terrible days of Nazism have been forgotten — '

'Not by me,' an old man with an ebony walking stick said suddenly, with fragile clarity.

'Mr Tenby will answer questions later.'

The little gnome bobbed up agitatedly.

'You want us to do a deal with the Germans,' the old man said.

'Yes,' said Tenby. He said it affably, as though welcoming an ally. 'We think that the stability of Europe depends on our doing a deal, as you put it, with Germany.'

'My oldest boy was killed in the First War, and the youngest in this last one.'

'A lot of our boys were killed in the wars,' said Tenby gravely. 'Many hideous things happened and a lot of mistakes were made. Many of us lost loved ones. But it will do us no good to sustain hatred year after year, decade after decade. How many more might we not lose in a war that broke out tomorrow? Far, far more. An ex-enemy has learnt from his mistakes and is working hard to build up a strong, free Europe. Are we going to refuse to co-operate because that country once did us wrong? There are forces active today which mean us a much greater wrong.'

The beautiful modulations soothed the heckler. He gave up, resting his weight on his stick and beginning to nod reluctantly, not so much convinced as hypnotized.

'I don't want anyone to think,' said Tenby, 'that when I speak in the House next week I shall be treating lightly the responsibilities which this country shouldered during and after the war. In past centuries there have been warring factions which recognized their true enemies in time and united against them. Sparta and Athens were in conflict until they saw the hordes of Persia coming against both of them . . . from the East. France and England were foes for almost a thousand years and then saw that they must stand shoulder to shoulder against the growing might of Germany.'

'It's all the same, then, isn't it?' The young man with the nuclear disarmament badge stood to one side, away from the ranks of the faithful. 'What was the good of fighting against France and slaughtering millions, century after century, only to find we were pals after all? Then going at the Germans — and now finding we're blood brothers.'

Tenby said condescendingly: 'Nobody is suggesting for a moment — '

'And what about the Japanese?' The

young man was shaky with nervousness but determined to go on. 'All that propaganda about the fiendish Japs — remember? Cartoons showing them as monkeys. Films and books about sadistic yellow bastards. And now every film and novel raves about them and their wonderful, age-old way of life.'

'Readjustment — '

'That's a useful word! Once we praised the Nazis because they were anti-Bolshie. Then the Russians were our gallant allies because they were anti-Nazi. We sent a volunteer force to fight with the Finns against the Russians, but when the Russians were on our side we forgot about the Finns and then later blamed them for letting Hitler take them over. China against the brutal Japanese . . . until it becomes the brutal Chinese and the civilized Japs. Where does it stop?'

Tenby's smile was patronizing in a way he would not have allowed it to be if he had not been conscious of his audience's support on this topic. He said meaningly:

'You are a member of the nuclear disarmament movement, I take it?'

'I am.' The young man stood erect as the girl came close and put her arm through his.

'One of the more — er — warlike members, by the sound of it.'

There was a titter of appreciation, sighing on the wind.

The young man said: 'When you've told the Germans they can keep their factories and make their own nuclear weapons and rely on us to fight with them if there's anyone they want to fight, what then? March against the Russians — or will it be the Chinese by then — or maybe the French? We've taken rather a dislike to the French again just recently. What is your policy towards the French . . . and, say, the Albanians?'

'Our policy,' said Tenby, 'is to present any potential invader with a deterrent. We cannot rely on American help for ever and in any case we wish to preserve our independence in matters of defence as in everything else.'

'If you're thinking along those lines do you support tomorrow's march to the American missile site at Whepgate? You ought to. You sound as though you're on our side. Come out into the open and say so.'

There were a few sympathetic laughs at this brave flourish, but they were drowned by a chorus of 'Go home . . . be your age . . . that's enough, son.'

Tenby went on speaking. He talked of associations of equal partners, of believers in democracy, of truth and freedom and the forgiveness of mortal injuries provided the injuries were past. Everything he said was valid. Nora felt prickles down her spine. All so true . . . yet flowering from such a dung-heap of accumulated, rotting treacheries. He was right, but for the wrong reasons.

'I say it again' — Tenby was building up to the sort of resonant magnificence that would earn him a round of applause — 'Europe must be united and each country must be allowed to retain its self-respect. No vengeance. No surliness. No recriminations. Our motives must be those of enlightened self-interest in some respects; in all respects of belief in freedom and mutual trust.'

'And personal profit,' said Nora loudly.

Tenby was undecided whether he faced a heckler or an ally. 'If by personal profit you mean — '

'I mean,' said Nora, 'that however plausible your motives may appear on the surface, not one of them has any bearing on the present situation.'

'Young lady — '

'Certain papers,' said Nora, waving a clutch of galley proofs supplied by Evan Downing, 'have come to the attention of less gullible people in London. Papers . . . ' She felt a tightness in her throat and knew how the shy, awkward nuclear disarmer had suffered, but forced himself to go on. She, too, went on. 'Papers,' she said, 'which raise interesting questions on how many of those most deeply concerned with Anglo-German integration have a personal financial stake in the result.'

There was a gasp. Tenby stood quite still for a moment, then said as lightly as possible: 'So they've sent a girl this time. A change from the gossip column, Miss . . . er . . . ?'

'Are you prepared to tell this audience how many acquaintances of yours hold a twenty per cent interest in Simeon Synthetics, which in turn nominally owns Cockaigne Plastics, which in turn is an affiliate of the Hartmann combine?'

One of the men by the house moved away from the wall and headed purposefully in her direction. Good. She must create enough trouble to get the others over here.

'And which Member of Parliament,' she cried out, 'was instrumental in smoothing the way for a forthcoming interchange of nuclear reaction information between Rheinhausen and Bentzon Vaughan?'

'Good for you!' breathed the young man fervently. His girl, leaning forward, nodded encouragingly.

'And isn't it true' — Nora edged away as the first man came at her and a second began to hurry down the lawn — 'that one of the most vocal spokesmen in the cause of delaying the dismantling of steel and chemical plant — Krupp factories, Hartmann factories, the lot — has for many years been an undeclared director of an English puppet company which was only waiting for the Common Market to become a reality? And when the Common Market was fluffed by you and your dimmer colleagues didn't he swing all his personal and business power into the Anglo-German alliance? What do you suppose his assets are worth today, Mr Tenby?'

They reached her. They had her by the arms and were suggesting in irritably reasonable voices that she should leave. The two nuclear disarmers began to laugh their delight. Nora could not have hoped for more valuable support. Heads turned towards them. A couple of people came to the assistance of the bouncers.

As the three of them were hustled out through the gates she hoped that the diversion had been enough; that Alan had been able to get into the house unnoticed.

5

The hall was deserted. Stairs rose in a right-angled turn to the landing above.

According to the glossy magazine they had consulted before setting out, Tenby's study was on the first floor at the far end of the landing where he would not be disturbed by passing footsteps when he was working. His bedroom opened out of it and there was a dressing-room between that and his wife's room. The study, according to photographs, commanded a fine view over the lawn and hedges through the trees to the tranquil stream and meadows at the bottom.

Alan went up the stairs. Not one of the treads creaked. He reached the top and went along the landing and into the passage at the end. The door of the farthest room was open. He was met by the smell of old books and papers, mingled with a cloying memory of cigar smoke.

There was a large desk with an armchair behind it. Two glass-fronted bookcases flanking the door caught ghostly reflections of the window and of himself moving against it.

He did not bother to try the desk drawers or investigate the squat cupboard in the corner. Tenby would not have left the evidence of his past lying about in unlocked drawers. It would be somewhere here; but somewhere very safe. Yet not so utterly and assuredly safe, they hoped, that Nora's outburst in the garden would fail to provoke Tenby into coming and checking when the meeting was over. Just a quick look . . . in spite of his certainty that the stuff must be here, that she was bluffing, half guessing . . . that no one could possibly have got at the documents.

Alan pulled one of the window curtains out from the wall. It was voluminous enough to conceal him when needed. He settled himself against the wall. He could have sat down but was not prepared to risk even the leathery whisper of a chair if he had to get out of it in a hurry. Long ago he had learnt to stand still. He had clung for twenty-four hours to one mountain ledge in a blizzard and knew how to huddle himself away from wind or cramp. Now he let his body relax and go half to sleep, his arms not moving, one hand in his pocket and the other against his chest. His shoulders drooped. He breathed slackly. He would wait all night if necessary.

Tenby might keep all the most dangerous papers in his bank. That meant that this whole effort was wasted. Or, in spite of Downing's views on Tenby's character, the stuff might have been destroyed years ago when the man switched his allegiance. But they had to try. If this failed they would have to try something else.

The afternoon light faded beyond the trees. The voices on the lawn died away into hollow echoes and then into silence. It was dark when at last there came the tread of footsteps along the corridor. The door opened and the light switch was snapped on. Tenby crossed the room to the desk and unlocked a drawer. It was impossible to see what he took out. Whatever it was, once he had found it he locked the drawer again. Then he stared towards the window.

Alan saw the blurred image of Tenby from an angle in the window-pane. He suddenly realized that he was in a vulnerable position. Now that evening was settling in, Tenby might well come to the window and draw the curtains. It would be the natural thing to do if he proposed to work for a little while in this room.

Alan tensed, ready for a fight here and now. Then the light went out and Tenby left the room.

Alan swiftly crossed to the door and opened it cautiously. Tenby had disappeared, but from the direction of the main landing came the sound of his footsteps, this time on a harder surface as though he were treading on wood or linoleum. Alan hurried after him and, past the head of the stairs, came to a narrower continuation of the carpeted staircase. Somewhere above, as he could plainly hear, was a flight of attic stairs.

He went up after Tenby.

The attic stairs were wide enough for one person at a time. At the top an open door shed a thin light down the wall. When Alan reached it he pressed himself against the wall and leaned forward.

Two old tables stood ranged under the sloping attic roof and at one end was a stack of trunks and cases. Tenby was bending over a large teak chest and unlocking it with what was presumably the key taken from the desk in his room.

He lifted the lid. Alan watched as he began to take out bundles of paper, each tied neatly with string. When he had stacked some twenty or so bundles beside him on the floor he stopped and peered into the chest. For a moment he contemplated the contents as though to imprint their solid reality on his memory.

'Charles . . . Charles, darling, what are you doing?'

Lighter footsteps were coming up the stairs. Tenby's head turned guiltily towards the door. Alan jerked back.

'Charles, what are you playing at up there?'

Alan sprang from the top step into the attic. Tenby, half expecting his wife but not prepared for her to come on him so suddenly, swung defensively away from the pile of papers. He was too late. He went under his own impetus into the swinging right that Alan aimed at his jaw, and sprawled to the bare boards. Alan turned back to the door, reaching round it to claim the key that had been left in the outer side.

Mrs Tenby's voice rose in agitation. 'Charles . . . '

Alan locked the door and went back to the open chest. Tenby lifted his head and tried to get up. Alan hit him again. This time Tenby stayed down.

There were four bulky envelopes on top of the mass of documents in the chest. They were labelled in a small pedantic script. As neat and formal and damning, thought Alan, as so much German material seized after the war — the same finicky insistence on retaining evidence against oneself, as though completeness of ledgers were a positive virtue in itself.

'Charles' — Mrs Tenby's voice was muffled but rising in shrillness — 'you've got to let me in. Do you hear me?'

Alan gathered up the envelopes. *Committee*, said one. *Putsch timetable*, said another blatantly. The German word had been used with the devotion of a child culling a vogue word from American films or a television series. Alan hitched the four envelopes under his left arm and went silently to the door. From the other side he could hear Mrs Tenby breathing with the suspicion of a throaty sob. When he turned the key in the lock she stopped.

He opened the door quickly.

She cried: 'Charles, if what that girl said — '

Then she screamed. He caught her by the arm and pulled her past him into the room. She stumbled and went down on her knees, saw her husband lying inert, and screamed again. Alan clattered away down the stairs, down the next flight, out on to the landing and down the main staircase. He reached the front door as a man in shirt sleeves emerged through a baize door at the side.

'Hey . . . '

Alan was out on the drive. He began to run. The man came after him. The drive wound away under the trees, the gateway lost in the night.

Then the car appeared. It reversed up the drive with a grinding roar that bounced back off the trees and started up echoes against some distant wall. Nora had the door swinging open as he reached it. He fell into the seat beside her. The man in pursuit grabbed the door and tried to hold it open while he reached for Alan. Nora started off in second gear and changed up to third with a shudder. The door forced the man inwards, his feet scrabbling along the ground. Alan hit him twice, and then the door was swinging free. Alan groped for it, pulled, and slammed it shut.

Nora put her foot down. They raced away from the gates, alongside the wall and the overhanging trees, and skidded right at the next crossroads.

'I'll take over now,' he said breathlessly.

As he hurried round to the driver's seat and Nora slid across, she reached down for the envelopes he had dumped at his feet.

'You really got the stuff?'

'It looks pretty authentic to me. We'll stop and have a good look when we reach the main road.'

He drove the Aston Martin forward, and the hedges streamed away behind. 'You know the direction?'

'I worked it out while I was waiting,' said Nora. 'This goes for about five miles in an arc and joins up with the main London road south of Cambridge. If they come after us — '

'They'll be too late,' said Alan. 'By the time Tenby comes round and starts a chase — if he's optimistic enough to do so — we'll be well on the way to London. His only chance would be to cut us off before we got into the main traffic. And I don't see how he'll do that, with the lead we've got.'

He felt the familiar steering wheel under his hands and the power of the car under his feet. From now on it was safe and easy. He accelerated, wanting to get away from the dark countryside to a place where they could settle down and study the papers he had stolen. They were certainly going to make fascinating reading.

They swung round a corner between ragged hedges; and suddenly there was no more road. It ran on for another fifty yards and then disappeared under a vast dark shape. There were two red lamps in the middle of the road.

Alan stamped on the brake. The car slid to a halt. Its headlights rested on what looked at first sight like a massive, toothy, red snow-plough.

It was a combine harvester. It completely blocked the way.

6

Nora said: 'But at this time of year . . . '

'It must have been on its way for an overhaul now that the season's over.'

Alan got out. The harvester's haunches squatted on either side of the narrow road. A man could squeeze past it against the hedge but there was no way of getting a car through.

Nora watched as he edged round one side and then reappeared from the other. Evidently no watchman had been left on duty.

'Impossible.' He came back to the car. 'Most effective road-block I've ever seen. It'd stop a tank.'

'I don't suppose they intend to use

tanks on us,' she said helplessly.

He slid back into the driver's seat and slewed the car in to the side. He backed, lurched forward, backed again. The wheels clawed at the grassy verge and on the fifth attempt they bumped over a hummock and were facing back in the direction from which they had come.

Nora felt a chill of fear — the first time she had been frightened today. The rest had been tense, alarming, and exciting, but some force within her had driven her on. Now that she had no further part to play but must simply sit here while Alan drove them back straight towards danger, she experienced something like the delayed shock that had hit her after the crash when she had first met Alan.

Fantastic, she thought, that he should now be sitting beside her, no longer a pursuer but a fugitive like herself. Her world had been tilted crazily. There was no safety in it any more.

'Those lights,' she said, suddenly alert. 'Are they on this road — coming this way?'

His hand stabbed at the dashboard and

the car was in darkness. They waited for another flicker through a distant hedge, down an incline a mile ahead. Alan said:

'They're on this road.'

'It's bound to be Tenby, isn't it?'

'We can hardly afford to wait and find out.'

He slowed, and on their right the bars of a gate broke the line of hedge. 'Open it,' said Alan urgently. She slid out of the car, fumbled with the cold iron latch, and humped the gate open. He drove past her and stopped, cutting his engine. Then he was handing her two of the bulky envelopes.

'Start walking.'

Nora said: 'We ought to stay near the car. Then, if it's not Tenby — '

'It's almost bound to be Tenby. The further away we are when he reaches that combine harvester, the better. He'll know we couldn't have passed him and we couldn't have driven any other way. He'll come looking.'

There was no panic in his manner. He was not discussing the situation: he was telling her with bleak logic what they must do. Nora felt a brief twinge of rebellion. She still wanted to cling to the belief that this was England and that violent, irrational things did not happen to people like herself. But when Alan began to stride away across the lumpy surface of the field, taking her obedience for granted, she found herself stumbling after him. They did not halt until they had reached the crown of a gentle slope. They had hardly been aware of walking uphill but the wind was stronger here. Beyond was a dark stain of trees flowing away towards the Suffolk border.

They crouched below a stunted pine on the edge of a plantation. Lights approached the barrier of the harvester on the road they had left. Voices drifted up as faint and tiny as the early-morning drowsiness of birds. Then torches raked across the field through a gap in the hedge and finally found the Aston Martin.

'Two or three of them,' murmured Alan. 'And there could be more, covering other roads, cutting us off.'

'But how could he dare to call anyone else in?'

Alan's hand on her arm drew her into the cover of the plantation. He said: 'Even if he hasn't got a private army he's got a tough set of drinking friends. You can bet that the boys of the local hunt are in his pocket. He could tell them about a robbery of state secrets — can't confide in the police, old boy, but I know I can rely on you. That kind of thing. Plus a few neo-Nazi types, probably like the one who killed my father. Boys of Tenby's kind command plenty of resources.'

They backed away through the trees, trying not to set twigs crackling explosively. When they came out on to coarse, tufted grass, Nora felt terrifyingly vulnerable. This was a bare, windswept country. Howling on the wind came the sound of a jet aircraft like a monster from some sinister local legend.

'We could go on all night,' she protested, 'and still not strike a good road — or at any rate one going in the right direction.'

'The right direction,' said Alan, 'is away from Tenby.'

Ahead of them another pair of bright

eyes looked over a slope and swung south. It could have been another car sent to cut them off. It could equally well have been an innocent traveller hurrying home.

Nora tripped and fell to her knee. Her foot twisted painfully in the hardening earth. She dropped the envelopes and groped for them.

Alan crouched beside her. 'Stay still for a moment.'

Two cars slowed to a halt a long way away. The beam of a torch flickered briefly up into the sky and then was snapped off by an irate hand. Ahead, two arms of coniferous woodland curved in but failed to meet. The light had stabbed up from the gap between them and now small dark figures moved across that gap.

'Tenby,' observed Alan wryly, 'has certainly called out a few of his chums.'

'If they know the countryside we don't stand a chance.'

'Come on.' Alan cut her peremptorily short. 'We can't stay here all night.' He stood up, inviting a cry of jubilant recognition. 'Let's cut down towards the far end of that copse. We might get round the trees to the road. There must be a road there: they've got their cars some-where along it. If we can keep well away from their parking place we'll pick up a signpost sooner or later.'

They resumed their uneven progress. Nora's breath shivered out of her with relief when they reached the comparative shelter of the copse. When they had skirted it they found themselves beside a straggling wire fence which led down a slope to what might be a road.

It was a road all right. They could hear no whisper of voices and see no lights. When they had climbed over a gate they came out into a winding lane. Alan nodded to the right and they began to walk that way. She hoped his instinct was reliable.

The land was almost flat yet the lane followed some twisting contour that brought them sometimes facing the wind, sometimes leaning away from it. They seemed to be pacing out some ancient boundary which would go on and on into the night without ever getting anywhere.

Reality was established once more by

the thrumming of the road surface beneath their feet. A heavy truck bore down on them, its light ablaze. Alan nudged Nora in to the side. It was useless to run. This must be what it felt like to be a rabbit trapped in the glare of headlights.

The truck jolted to a stop.

'Going some place? Care for a ride?'

From this range the American military markings on the mudguards were visible. The driver's face was a pallid, elongated moon poking out over the door.

'We'd be glad of one.'

'Climb up and join me. Here, lady, take a hold.'

Alan helped Nora up into the cab and then swung in beside her. The driver emitted a grunt that might have expressed discomfort or approval.

The truck rumbled forward. Branches from the roadside whipped the side of the cab.

'Goin' as far as Whepgate. The camp. Okay with you if I shed you in the village?'

'Couldn't be better,' said Alan.

Nora leaned against his shoulder and

he put his arm round her. She immediately wanted to go off to sleep although this could only be early evening. Or was it, by now, the middle of the night? She had lost track of time and everything that was rational and proper. But they ought to be all right now. Nobody would stop an American vehicle.

'If you want to be put down some place else, before we get to Whepgate — '

'Whepgate will do splendidly, thank you,' Alan assured him.

'There ain't nowhere between here and there anyway,' the driver ruminated. 'Not so's you'd notice, that is.'

The lane straightened and splayed out to a T-junction. And suddenly the driver was saying: 'Hey, get that, will ya?' and touching his brakes.

A small signpost stood in a grass triangle in the middle of the junction. Its arms were obscured by haversacks and what looked like a couple of guitars. The grass there and up the low banks was almost obliterated by people sprawled out on blankets and groundsheets.

'They ain't supposed to be squattin'

until tomorrow,' said the driver in an aggrieved tone.

Two young men sprang from the sides of the road and faced into the oncoming headlights. Behind them, others spread across the road and sat down, blocking the way.

The driver cursed, stopped, and leaned out of the cab. 'Look, clear this road, will ya?'

'You're heading for Whepgate Camp?'

'That's right.'

'We're not going to let you through,' said the young man pleasantly.

'Look, son — you can start demonstrating all you want tomorrow. Just let me drive through. It's nothing to do with me, any of it — honest.'

'Nothing to do with you? You work for a system that can sling weapons into the air like toys to kill people you've never even met, and you say it's nothing to do with you?'

'Look, bud — '

'All those missiles you've got over at Whepgate will be fired one day. Like children with dangerous toys, you'll have to use them just to see what kind of a bang they make.'

The driver writhed in exasperation. 'I've got an itch in my foot,' he confided to Alan. 'It'd be just great to lift it off the brake and drive right through those mugs.'

'You see what our young friend means,' said Alan, 'by dangerous toys in impatient hands.'

'Say, what kind of talk is that? I give you a ride and you start siding with these nuts against me.'

'Sorry.' Alan touched Nora's arm. 'I think we'd better get out.'

'Listen,' said the driver, solemnly conscious of his own charitable nature, 'I'll have to turn and drive round this. If you care to stick with me I'll get us through somehow.'

'If they're not littering all the other approaches.'

'Hell, they can't lay siege to the whole area.'

'They can try.'

Nora felt Alan slip away from her and open the door of the cab. He held up his right hand as he got down. She rested her fingertips lightly on it and sprang down beside him. The truck backed away and twisted in to the verge. When the driver had wrenched it round he drove off in a rattle of impatience, the red tail light disappearing round the long curve of the lane.

The young man said: 'I say, I'm sorry you got caught up in this. I didn't realize you weren't from the camp.'

'Now that you've landed us here,' said Alan, 'perhaps you can tell us the way to the nearest place of any size where we can hire a car or find a railway station.'

Somewhere in the background a girl giggled. Faces like the distorted faces of trolls peered out from the darkness. There were girls wearing dark blue hoods several sizes too large for them, young men with knitted woollen bonnets dragged down over their ears, and some who had let their hair grow long enough to serve as headgear.

The young man said: 'This country isn't too well served with public transport. Whepgate is down the road there, but you won't find anything in it but a decrepit old church and a pub. The pub will have a telephone, I suppose, but you'll have quite a job getting anyone from civilization to come out here at this time of the evening.'

The wind soughed above them. Nora was conscious of great spaces above and around, of interminable fields and undulating land running on to the edge of the world. The road was unsteady beneath her feet. The earth reeled. She reached for Alan's arm and held on to it; and the world steadied.

She asked: 'What do you hope to gain by hanging about here all night and then sitting down outside the barbed wire? That is, I suppose they have barbed wire.'

'They have barbed wire,' the young man agreed chattily. 'And we'll sit down there and they'll drag us away. Some of us will get fined and a few of us will get slung in clink. Disturbers of the peace — that's us. As though the greatest potential disturbers of the peace aren't those things on the other side of the barbed wire!'

'But what will you achieve?'

'Frankly, I don't know. We try things without knowing if they'll deflect the course of history by a thousandth of an inch. But we do try. We have to try.'

Further along the road someone began to sing softly to the running chords of a guitar.

'Thanks for condemning us to a long walk,' said Alan. 'I'm sure it'll be good for us.'

'Sorry about that, but — '

'In war,' Alan took him up, 'you have to be ruthless. Isn't that it?'

'I wouldn't put it quite like that.'

'The parallel seems a fair one to me,' said Alan. 'But never mind. Good night.'

He and Nora took the left turning at the junction and walked along the slightly widening road towards Whepgate.

The marchers had spread a considerable distance. They lay in small groups at the roadside and thickened into a sociable cluster near the whitewashed wall of what must once have been a schoolhouse, now abandoned. A girl's clear voice drifted out through the black yawn of a window that had long since lost its glass.

    'We'll sit on our bottoms until the
      day
    They take the nuclear warheads
      away,
    And march along with our hands in
      our pockets
    Until they get rid of their murder-
      ous rockets . . . '

Several voices took up a blurred refrain.

Light stabbed suddenly through a hedge at the corner Alan and Nora had just left behind. At once he was gripping her arm and steering her swiftly towards the school gate and up an overgrown path to the door. They stumbled over an uneven flagstone and then were inside.

Somebody laughed in the blackness. In the next room the singing wavered up to a peak, then a sleepy voice said: 'Save it for the morning,' and there was a brief, drowsy argument.

Headlights swept through the window gap and across the opposite wall. Faces turned resentfully up from the floor.

'Aren't we ever going to get any peace?'

'Did we have to get here so early anyway? I mean, I don't mind being a martyr tomorrow — that's what I've come for — but I'd sooner have kept the wind out of my drawers tonight.'

'Is that all you want to keep out?'

There was a subdued, laughing scuffle in a corner of the room. Nora tripped over someone's leg, and then Alan guided her to the wall. They slid down to the cold floor. There was a smell of chill stone and rotting woodwork.

Close to Nora's ear someone said: 'You two got a blanket?'

'We've just got here,' said Alan. 'We'll manage.'

'Here — we each brought one, but we seem to be sharing.'

'Clive, honest, the way you talk . . . '

The blanket was passed across to them in the gloom, lit only by a faint haze from outside that was not moonlight. Nora was thankful to roll on to the blanket. Exhaustion came over her in a wave.

A fretful spark of brilliance bobbed like a firefly or the reflection from a jogging glass across the ceiling and down one wall. In one corner a man began to snore. In the next room there was a sleepy purr of conversation. There were other voices, too: purposeful, wideawake voices. They came closer to the building and footsteps left the overgrown playground and hit the flagged floor of the schoolhouse.

Light stabbed out again. This time it came in a narrow beam slashing round the room next door and cutting across the open connecting doorway.

'What's the idea?'

'Raiders, boys. It's an ambush!'

There was a stir of disgruntled activity. The footsteps went inexorably round the room. The rectangle of the doorway was suddenly sharp-edged and a man in an overcoat stood in it.

Nora felt Alan roll suddenly close to her. He pushed the envelopes between them, making a lumpy mattress. His left hand was on her shoulder and his mouth was against her cheek. 'Make it convincing,' he murmured. His mouth travelled across her cheek and found her lips. She caught at the edge of the blankets and pulled it over his shoulders as he let his full weight fall on her.

7

Alan felt through his left elbow the movement of the sagging floor as the men came into the room. And beneath him he felt Nora's instinctive movement of protest . . . and then the relaxation as she accepted the role she had to play.

The beam of the torch scoured the room. In here the indignant voices were louder. 'What the hell do you think this is? . . . Third degree now, by the look of it . . .'

A girl began to chant croakily the chorus of an anti-bomb song, but someone told her to shut up. It was not one of the intruders who had spoken: they were contemptuously silent.

Alan lifted his mouth from Nora's and then let it sink again. Her hand crept round his head. As the full light of the torch shone down on them she began to ruffle his hair.

The beam stayed on them.

Alan opened his lips. Nora's mouth opened and she simulated a convincing moan.

'Get out of here, will you?' said a man aggressively from the far side of the room. 'We can do without Peeping Toms. Flashlight photographs barred. Go on — clear off.'

The torch flicked away, perhaps to pick him out. Then the feet stamped out of the room, followed by a chorus of jeers.

Alan stayed where he was. Nora's fingers on the back of his neck had been tense, the nails digging into his flesh. Now the tautness had gone out of her hand but it was not moving away. She turned her head so that her mouth escaped his, but when he pursued she yielded to him again. He brought his left hand up to her throat and touched first the coldness of the throat and then the warmer flesh beneath.

Nora murmured: 'You needn't make it so convincing. They've gone away.'

'I know.'

'Alan . . . '

He silenced her again with his lips and moved so that his hand had more freedom. Twice she turned her head to escape and twice he reclaimed her. When she tried to whisper a protest he put his cheek against hers — warmer now — and said: 'It's an old custom. Didn't you know? People have always made love when fleeing from danger. Must be the life force asserting itself in the face of imminent death, if you want to get philosophical about it. Which I don't.'

'We're not in danger of death.'

'I wouldn't be too sure.'

But he was not thinking of death. Confidently he explored her body, bringing it to life in tune with his own.

Someone hummed softly in the next room. Here there was no sound but the rustle of his arm against the blanket and the quickening of Nora's breath.

'Not here,' she pleaded suddenly, vainly. 'Not in this place. Not like this. Not now.'

'Here,' he said. 'Like this. Now.'

He moved suddenly, and banged his head against the hard wall. Nora laughed softly in the darkness. A few seconds later she laughed again, but it was an excited laugh now — the laughter of exultation and acceptance.

8

'So it's you!' said the young man in the grey sweater. He reached out and grabbed his girl friend's arm, hauling her closer. 'Look, Francie. I was sure it was. You remember.'

'Yes,' said Francie. 'I remember.'

They were walking through the cold morning air towards Whepgate. The young man who had tried to heckle Tenby fell into step beside Nora and looked his undoubted approval; but whether that approval was governed mainly by her own attack on Tenby the previous day or by her appearance, it was impossible to decide.

The young man was called Bertrand. He showed his pride in this by making three jokes in ten minutes about a certain other eminent anti-bomb demonstrator of the same name. His girl friend tried to keep abreast for a while, but finally dropped behind, leaving Alan, Nora, and Bertrand in a row while she trudged along on her own, the low hard heels of her sandals slapping against the road. She had a pretty face with dark eyelashes and a leisurely pouting lip. Her black hair hung down like heavy curtains on both sides.

A scurrying little man made his way forward through the marchers until he had come level with Bertrand. When introduced to Nora and Alan he studied them suspiciously.

'Weren't with us when we started out.'

'But we're glad to have them with us,' said Bertrand.

'You want to watch 'em.' He made no attempt to lower his voice.

His name was Joey. He was smaller than Bertrand and did not look as generous. He had the air of a townsman, glaring at every gap in the hedges as though fearing the emergence of some unidentifiable animal. He suspected the existence of fifth columnists among the marchers and was obviously prepared to classify Alan and Nora as such at first sight.

'Nice morning,' said Bertrand blithely, to nobody in particular.

'That ground was damp last night,' said Joey. 'Came right through my groundsheet. I can feel it right up my back.'

'Nice and warm in the cells tonight,' said Bertrand.

'Ha, ha,' said Joey mirthlessly.

Ahead of them the leaders of the column struck up a disorganized song which gradually solidified into a jingle about the bluebells blooming 'neath the bomb blast.

Nora put out her hand. Alan took it. Life had been strange in recent years, but none of it had seemed as strange as this simple nonsense of holding a girl's hand as they walked along a country road in this odd company. It was incongruously more disturbing than their fierce discovery of one another in the darkness of the night; and yet, like that, it was absolutely right.

They mounted a small incline. From here they could see a spattering of squat white buildings below. The marchers slowed. There was a huddle at the top of the slope like an advance guard assembling for consultation before pressing on towards the battlefield.

Joey shifted his weight from one foot to the other. 'Look, this is the last time as far as I'm concerned. Next time I'm staying with the sit-downers in Trafalgar Square. At least you know where you are. This place . . . ' Words failed him. He waved despairingly at the countryside.

Alan drew Nora away and studied the landscape. Two or three miles away was a railway line, and at one spot a white blur that might be a level-crossing. There was no station in sight but there must be one somewhere beyond the low hump of land behind which the line vanished.

Nora said: 'Is this where we leave the pilgrims?'

'We want a telephone, a train and the quickest route to London.'

He helped her over the nearest gate.

Nobody paid much attention except Joey, who wagged his head knowingly, and Francie, who suddenly ran after them. 'Here' — she fumbled in a capacious pocket and took out a crumpled plastic string bag. It belonged in the Fulham Road on a Saturday morning rather than here on a Sunday. 'I don't know what you're doing,' she said, 'but whatever it is you don't want to lug those envelopes along under your arm all the time. Go on — take it.'

Alan packed the envelopes in, stretching the strands, and then they set off down the rough field and up the slope of the knoll beyond. Ahead of them was another gentle undulation, ending in the wall of a pine wood. The grass was like a vast scrubbing-brush underfoot. A few shrivelled purple flowers were like dry paper in the stubble.

They reached the dark wood and went along one of its cold aisles. There were jagged stumps to trip them up and twisted branches as pliable and harsh as wire to scratch them. When they came out of the eerie green twilight into the open once more they were above a narrow ditch cut deeply into the ground.

'Look!' gasped Nora.

Their pursuers had outflanked them. They were spread out in a thin line like beaters across the open country. Swinging round in an arc, they were preparing to head for the wood.

Alan and Nora backed away into the trees.

Alan jerked his head towards the eastern end of the wood. It ran along the low ridge and down to within a few hundred yards of the nuclear missile encampment. Using its shelter they could get close to the camp. There was no other safe route.

Nora choked back a sob. The sight of those men out there, advancing like moving scarecrows on the wood, had hit her hard. Alan wanted to hold her hand again, but progress between the trees would have been impossible.

'Nearly there,' he said encouragingly as they floundered through the ankle-deep tangle that clutched at them and tried to tip them over.

They reached the lower tip of the wood. It narrowed almost to a point here. Across the stretch of open land ahead was the camp, which on the surface consisted only of a few huts and three long, low brick buildings like squashed hangars.

The pursuers were crunching in amongst the trees.

Nora said: 'We'll never make it. We can't just dash — '

'Whatever tricks they decide to play,' said Alan, 'they're hardly likely to risk shooting at us.'

They could not hope to cross that open space undetected. It was a matter of plucking up courage and running. And there was still no guarantee that they would be any safer when they reached the barbed-wire perimeter of the camp. Already there was trouble enough over there.

The marchers had just reached the main gate. Some spread groundsheets on the road and sat down. Others formed a small barrier outside the gate, facing inwards. They were evidently expected. A truck at once ran along the main camp road to the gate. The gate was opened and one of the sentries said something to the knot of people outside, who refused to move.

As though at a prearranged signal, two lorries came into view along the road which the marchers had followed. They drew up a few yards from the outer fringe of blankets and groundsheets. Policemen dropped over the railboards. An inspector strode along the ragged lines of squatters, exhorting them to get up and go away.

Alan said: 'Right. Let's be off.'

They broke from the shelter of the trees and ran towards the camp.

From behind them there came a shout. In front there was also, now, a great deal of shouting. Orders were barked out and the police began to advance in groups, picking their way between the irregular huddles of young men and women on the ground. Two of them stooped at one point and picked up a girl by her shoulders and legs.

Nora and Alan proceeded across the uneven ground in leaps and stumbling hops.

Nobody at the camp saw them coming: they were all too thoroughly occupied. Several men had lifted the wire and crawled through. They began to run across the flat central area of the camp, a featureless rectangle like some vast, deserted parade-ground. Soldiers emerged from two of the huts and sprinted to cut them off. When they reached the leader of the small invading party he promptly sat down. While two of them laboriously heaved his dead weight off the ground, another of the intruders dashed for a nearby hut and pinned a notice to the door. It was promptly torn down.

Alan and Nora lurched in the wake of the police into the middle of the crowd and slumped down on the road. They were treated to a couple of curious glances but no one questioned their right to be there.

The police were carrying their captives bodily towards the lorries and loading them aboard. They picked and chose among the sitters, seeming to know the ringleaders.

At last Nora allowed herself to look

back the way they had come. Alan followed the direction of her gaze and saw three men striding towards the demonstration. One was in an overcoat, the other two in short khaki raincoats. A police sergeant on his way back from a lorry stopped them and asked a curt question. One of them leaned confidentially towards him. The sergeant listened and nodded, respectful now.

Alan stuck out his feet. The police inspector, waving two of his men forward, tripped and regained his balance with difficulty. He licked his lips hopefully.

'Bright lot of pacifists!' he said loudly to no one in particular. 'Violence now, eh?'

He glared at Alan's leg, still sprawled out in full view. He took a step back. Then a tinge of surprise came into his expression.

'Aren't you a bit old for this sort of thing, sir? I mean this is for kids, not for the likes of you.' He took in Nora as well and his opinion was confirmed. 'I'd have thought folks like you 'ud know better.'

Alan stayed where he was, his head

tilted back. He produced a scornful smile for the inspector's benefit. There was only one safe way out of this place now. A bit rough, maybe, but safe . . . if it worked.

The scornful smile did not appeal to the inspector, but reluctantly he said: 'Now, look — what say you give me your name and address and then clear off? You've made your point. You've done your demonstration.' Two of his men bumped into him as they shuffled past with a heavy youth dangling between them. 'We've got our difficulties, sir,' said the inspector, undoubtedly wondering if these two people were well-known and well-respected citizens who might direct unwelcome publicity on him if he didn't tread carefully. 'Come on, now — you look a reasonable sort.'

There came a shout from the edge of the group. 'Not them — don't waste your time on them!'

It was Joey. He was squatting close to the barbed wire, watched with weary amusement by two Americans on the other side. Nobody was making any move to arrest him. One policeman actually stepped over him with great care.

'They're fakes!' shouted Joey indignantly.

The two men in raincoats left the police sergeant and came on through the crowd. They might have been taken for plain-clothes men on duty. Even the inspector might have thought they were colleagues.

Desperately Nora pushed herself up into a half-kneeling position. She needed no prompting. Her quick, nervous smile at Alan told him that she, too, had recognized the escape route. She shouted:

'It's no use, Inspector. We're not going to be intimidated.'

'I'm not trying to intimidate you. And you don't have to shout at me. I'm just telling you for your own good — '

'What do you know about goodness, Inspector?'

'Don't listen to her!' Joey had got up of his own accord and was threading his way towards them. 'They're not genuine. You can't arrest them — they don't belong to us.'

The inspector bent over Nora; and she

knocked his cap off.

There was a moan of outrage from the sitters nearby.

'You see?' howled Joey. 'I told you. That's no way to behave. That's not non-violent. They're not ours at all.'

A constable bent over Nora and got his hands under her armpits. Another hurried to his assistance. The two men in raincoats were getting nearer, examining each face that they passed. Alan got to his feet and grabbed the arm of the nearer constable. 'Let her go.' The policeman tried to shake him off. Alan held on. A moment later he was pulled off by a third constable.

'You realize what you've done?' puffed the third, as Alan and Nora were loaded on to a lorry, Nora clinging to the string bag. 'It's Sunday today, right? The magistrate won't see you till tomorrow. You'll have to be shut up till morning, the lot of you — spread out over all the local gaols. You know what you've done?'

The tailboard was fastened up and the lorry drew away with a full load. Alan looked back at the two men who stood by the roadside apart from the crowd, to be joined by a third in an overcoat. Joey also stood to one side, equally irate.

'Yes,' said Alan tranquilly, 'we know what we've done.'

9

The magistrate said: 'A man of your reasonably mature years ought to set a better example.'

He was a tall man who sat with his head lowered between bony shoulders. His spectacles had wide black rims and behind them his eyes were pale and elusive. He dealt swiftly and gleefully with a succession of anti-nuclear demonstrators — a fine here, a month's imprisonment there, dealt out like the slash of a whip.

'Quite apart from causing an obstruction on the highway and indulging in conduct likely to lead to a breach of the peace,' he said to Alan, 'you wilfully obstructed a police officer when in the execution of his duty.' He waited, possibly hoping that Alan would produce an argument on which he could pounce. Alan remained silent. The magistrate went on: 'If I were to regard your action as an assault, rather than merely resistance or obstruction, I could be very severe on you indeed.'

If he was now waiting for an abject apology or an appeal for clemency he was going to be unlucky. Alan's hatred rose within him, but he knew better than to lay himself open to the spitefulness of a man of this calibre. The cat was tempting the mouse to be either defiant or humble. Silence was the only worthy response. Alan wanted the charade to be ended so that he could finish the job that had kept him too long in England already and then be free of it all. He was tired of self-righteous faces like the face of this man on the bench; tired of the easy platitudes and the prissy regulations and the smug denunciations. This present charge, against him and all the others, was irrelevant to the huge reality of what was going on in the world and to what he and Nora had been doing; yet to the man with the long face and the policemen in court it was in some way divinely ordained. The rules had always been there for them, the petty little rules governing their petty little lives. Take a hundred lines . . . ten strokes of the cane . . . a parking ticket . . . fine of ten pounds . . . two months' imprisonment without the option . . .

The pettiness of England nauseated him. He wanted to be out of here and out of the country, away on his own.

But he was no longer alone. Nora was beside him.

'As you have no previous convictions, I am prepared to be lenient. You will pay a fine of five pounds.'

Nora also paid five pounds. They left the court together. When they were out in the open air she swayed and leaned against him.

He said: 'The miserable little bastard.'

'I wanted to throw up,' said Nora.

Then she stood upright, her fingers plucking at his arm. Together they saw the car on the other side of the road. The man in the raincoat who had been leaning against the door said something to a man inside. Nora's hand tightened on the shopping bag and it swung against Alan's leg.

The man began to cross the road, ready to intercept them at the foot of the wide steps. Then he stopped as another car slid across his path and halted at the kerb.

The back door of the Bentley opened. Evan Downing said: 'Come on. Get in.'

Nora almost fell into the car. Alan followed her in, and the Bentley drew away. Behind them the man in the road turned and hurried back to his friend.

Downing glanced up in the driving mirror. 'Those are the boys?'

'They're the ones,' Alan agreed.

'They'll probably come after us, Fred,' Downing said to the driver.

'They'll find it tough going,' said the driver happily. 'And they'd better not start anything.'

Alan let himself sink back against the soft leather. He felt no further apprehension about their pursuers. Tenby had lost the game now.

Downing, half slewed round in the

front seat, said: 'And you've really got the stuff?'

Nora began to laugh shakily. She went on until Alan put his hand over hers. Then she went limp and said: 'All last night I was afraid they'd find some way — that they'd report these envelopes as stolen property and come looking for us.'

It had been present in Alan's mind also. But somehow he had been unable to visualize Tenby organizing an open enquiry from one police station to another. If Tenby had been asked for a description of the missing items, and then asked to establish ownership, he could soon have been pulled in deeper than he would have wished to go.

'The risk of letting us get away,' Nora marvelled. 'Surely he could have thought of something. Even now, isn't there a chance . . . ?'

'Maybe he's past it,' said Alan. The car hummed down the miles to London and there was no sign of a pursuer. 'Maybe,' he said, 'it's got past that. He'll have to make new plans — very different ones.'

'Let me see,' Downing begged, like a

small boy eager to open his Christmas stocking. 'Pass me a bit of the loot and let me make sure it's the real thing.'

Nora took one of the envelopes from the bag and handed it to him. With trembling fingers he unfastened it.

As they approached the outer suburbs Alan knew with a dark, disturbing knowledge that the journey was in fact not yet over. He had set out to do more than just provide a newspaper proprietor with a collection of incriminating documents.

The words were forced out of him. 'Tenby's got to die.'

Beside him he felt Nora jump.

'Wonderful.' Downing crackled a sheaf of papers and nodded lovingly over them. 'There's not much doubt about this.' Then he realized that Alan was owed at least a polite response to his remark. 'We can do a lot with this — but I doubt whether it's enough to get Tenby convicted of your father's murder. We may have our own views on the subject, but at a murder trial they want pretty substantial evidence. I don't see that we've got enough to — '

'Somehow,' said Alan, 'he has to die.'

'He'll be ruined. I'll see to that.'

'Ruined,' said Alan. 'Slapped down in one place, yes . . . but with the support of his precious friends he can build up again, somewhere else. His stocks and shares can be shifted. A job will be found for him. They don't stop flourishing, men like that, unless they are cut down. Exposure isn't enough. The scorn of other people isn't enough, since they will only be people Tenby has always despised anyway. A man with his own paid killers, fooling the community and using the resources of that community against the truth . . . Evidence or no evidence, he is too corrupt to live.'

Only an hour ago they had been standing in a courtroom while the processes of law had been applied to them. It was a law which found it easy to deal with cases of obstruction but not with murder; a law framed to irritate the many and spare the powerful few; a strange legal mesh that trapped innumerable small fry yet somehow let the big ones get through. A man like Tenby would know how to wriggle free. He might be accused of many things now in Downing's newspapers, but he would survive. He would disappear from public life for a while but would continue to live and scheme.

Tenby is more dangerous than my father ever was, thought Alan. Philip Sengall had been a poor misguided fanatic who believed every word he uttered. He never wavered, never went back on his original principles, evil as they might have been. Once you knew what Sengall's terms of reference were, you knew the danger he represented. But Tenby was the full-time English hypocrite — the trimmer, the suave evader, the man whose only guiding principle was the preservation of his own way of life at whatever cost to the country and people he claimed to serve. It was the Tenbys who needed stamping out because they were so much more insidious. Bacteria were more to be dreaded than tigers.

Alan had accepted a challenge from Nora Downing. It had taken him further than he would have wished to go but there was no turning back now. He had always finished any job he tackled before moving on.

He said: 'We know what Tenby has done. Legal proof or no legal proof, we know what he must have done. And if you mean well to your country you must know that he's got to be got rid of. My job, as I see it, isn't finished until he's dead.'

4

Traitor's Voice

1

Charles Tenby glanced down at his notes although he knew them off by heart. Then he looked steadfastly across the House. There were few gaps of green leather to be seen. The ranks were tightly packed and the big guns would be in position over there.

The enemy was not only on the Opposition benches. He had many others on this side of the House. The split on the Anglo-German question was not a party split. The official Government line made many of its own supporters uneasy.

There had been two or three catalytic moments in Tenby's life before now. Some men didn't see such moments coming and recognized opportunity only when it had passed them by. In politics of all things it was essential to be farsighted. He had always had the flair. The people who hated him most were those who most envied him this gift.

What none of them appreciated was that his intuition was in no way linked with personal greed. He had always been loyal to his concept of England. His distinguished career was a testimony to his integrity. It *had* been distinguished. Whatever dirt might be thrown at him an hour or two from now, he would not waver in his conviction that he had acted for the best. Hundreds in this House and millions outside would not understand. Such people had always been wrong and always would be wrong.

Desine de quoquam quicquam bene velle mereri . . .

A voice trailed away and heads turned expectantly.

The Speaker called him.

Charles Tenby rose. His left hand moved smoothly up to his lapel. He smiled, half inviting others to share the joke at his predictability. He was one of the great figures in the House — great and inimitable.

He said: 'I beg to move that this House do take immediate steps to implement the draft Treaty of Alliance between this country and the German Federal Republic . . .'

There had been no further instalment of Sengall's memoirs in any of Downing's papers. The veiled threats which that girl in his garden had levelled at him must all have been bluff. But Downing's hirelings, the scum of Fleet Street, now had the documents and would somehow make use of them. Today or tomorrow he would be challenged in the Press and here. The Opposition would be down on the revelations with howls of glee.

He faced them and went on with the words that were right and true and sensible. All they had to do was listen. Any reasonable man would be persuaded.

'Germany today stands for all that we, too, stand for in Europe and the civilized world. Let us not lose sight of that. Whatever prejudices some of us may still hold, let us recognize the realities of the world today.

'Many distinguished historians with access to a growing body of documents regarding the origin of the Second World War have come round to the view that its outbreak was a ghastly blunder. Neither side intended to fight. Many people believed then, and *know* now, that Bolshevism is our ultimate enemy. I will say frankly that up to the outbreak of war, and even later, I took that view myself. I am still convinced of its justice.' He went on swiftly, cutting his way through the threatening growl that rose from the benches opposite. 'When it was clear that, because of tragic errors, Hitler's Germany had got out of hand, I threw all my efforts into the overthrow of that regime. Today I consider it my duty to put the same effort into supporting the new Germany against the unchanging enemy — Bolshevism.'

There were some shouts from the Opposition, but as yet no scathing, specific questions. Unco-ordinated heckling meant nothing to an experienced speaker.

Tenby went on: 'This country has had many setbacks in its dealings with the Common Market countries. Nevertheless we continue to believe in Europe as an entity — perhaps more sincerely, in spite of our reservations, than some of its most vociferous supporters do. The country that has most often held out its hand to us during years of negotiation and discussion has been Germany. The time has come when both countries see that it will be to their mutual advantage to form a close military, economic, and technological alliance. No other existing treaties will be broken because of this; but the two major nations of Europe will from now on think and act in partnership, giving a lead to all others.'

He might have to resign. If the *Mercury* printed extracts from those documents (and he thought Downing fully capable of risking libel and all other dangers, given such a shield) his career could be ruined.

Resign.

There would always be a job for him somewhere. After the howls of execration had died down there would be intelligent men to agree that his valuable training must not be wasted . . . his own associates who would look after him . . .

Resign.

But he belonged here.

It was his duty to stay on. He was devoted enough and sure enough of himself to go on even when there was the danger of an ungrateful country turning on him and spitting on him.

History would understand, as it understood so many things. If he failed the failure would be a noble one. Nobler than Hitler's. In the long run Hitler had not been a great man. He had lacked the stamina and the breeding, the intuitive good taste, the intelligence based on wide education and a civilized social background.

The whole story must be told now, here in the House, before any garbled version came out.

Courage, his wife had said. He must tell them, she had insisted, and they would see. Now as ever, she gave him her trust and support. She believed in him and what he stood for. He could look back with pride on his childhood and youth, on Eton and Benedict's, on his arduous work on behalf of Anglo-German friendship at a crucial time, on his loyalty to his country right or wrong, and now his unflagging devotion to the cause of Anglo-German friendship once more. He had never sought personal success: that had come as an unexpected reward. He was a patriot in the truest sense. He knew what was best for England. He had always known.

'Before I tell the House what recommendations we have for establishing closer bonds between British and German industry and defence forces,' he said, 'I have a personal statement to make.'

There had been the beginnings of restlessness. Now there was a hush. A personal statement could be an ominous thing. The Member must not, according to Parliamentary usage, be questioned on it. It was taken that he would tell the truth on some matter which he felt it necessary to raise, and that there would be no further discussion. They could tell from his tone of voice that something extraordinary was coming. Of course they could. He knew his job, which was to make them listen. Given the opportunity all those years ago he would have made the entire country listen — and then, too, there would have been no answering back. Perhaps it was still not too late.

He said: 'However sincere one may be, there are always people only too ready to make mischief by picking on insignificant details and inflating them out of all proportion. The statesman must be continually on his guard against such threats. This last weekend I found myself involved in a misunderstanding of which I had previously had no glimmering what-soever. It was drawn to my attention, to my great distress, that certain investments which I and my family had held for a long time — investments made in the usual way through reliable brokers who had innocently not considered any remote political implications — were in fact tied up in a very roundabout way with certain Continental holdings. My conscience on this subject is clear. The ramifications of the various companies in which I had invested were unknown to me and it would not have occurred to me that they might in due course give rise to embarrassment either to me or to the cause which I serve.' Laughter welled up faintly from the other side. The respect extended to a personal statement could not entirely subdue the more raucous elements. Tenby braced his shoulders back and raised his voice. 'I wish to make it clear to this House that as soon as I was put in possession of the facts I took immediate steps to dispose of all such holdings. My broker has been instructed to sell these investments. As I have said, my conscience is clear, but no personal concern must impede my freedom to speak out, freed from encumbrances, on the matters which are of such vital concern to us today.'

It had been hard. Having built up so much, it had been painful to throw it away. But the substance was still there. The house was there, his wife was there, the children were alive and well and would never be poor. All of it had been worth the struggle. He had nothing to be ashamed of. He was faintly proud of the suspicion of tears in his voice when he said:

'I had to ensure when I rose to speak to you today that it would be without the faintest shadow of personal gain lying across what I said.'

'Making a profit on the deal?' jibed someone, unable to keep it in any longer. There was a babble of confused derision.

The Speaker called for order. 'Members must allow me to hear this. If the Right Honourable Member is declaring an interest it is essential that I should know.'

Tenby said: 'I no longer have any interest to declare. I have disposed of everything which might impede my freedom of action at this time. All else that I have to admit on my own behalf is something of which I am not ashamed. I make no secret of my feelings towards Germany before the war. There are men in this House and outside it who felt as I did and who still feel as I do. We were inspired only by love of our country. Slanderous imputations may now be cast on our behaviour. Malicious elements in every community seek to tear down those who have been consistently devoted to one clear cause. But we do not flinch. A group of distinguished men to which I once belonged . . . ' He told them obliquely as much as it was necessary for them to know.

There was silence now. His spirits rose. They were accepting his explanations and would seek no further. If any awkward questions should come up he would circumvent them on a plea of privilege. He understood the subtleties of Parliamentary privilege better than any of them — better, he suspected, than the Speaker himself.

It was time now to switch from the personal to the general. He outlined the Government's proposals for the smoother exchange of raw materials, finished goods, and technical information and for the easier registration of Anglo-German trading combines and manufacturing groups.

He had done so much for England and so little of it would ever be appreciated.

He had wanted to build his country into the same pattern as his own life. The graciousness of his home and his whole existence, the civilized conversation, the fine things and the awareness of finer things . . . There could be no finer pattern. Because there must be no flaw in it he had eliminated Sengall. Sengall was like those men on the benches opposite and like some of the more repulsive ones surrounding him right at this moment. They asked to be trodden on, like beetles invading your beautiful home.

He tried not to let the beetles see his contempt, but he sensed that they had already turned against him. The comparative silence in which his speech was being received was due not to slothful acceptance but to cold hostility. They were not shouting disapproval, since his arguments were flawless and unanswerable and they had nothing with which to refute them. But in due course they would find ways of opposing him simply for the sake of opposing him.

Logic was not enough. Common sense meant nothing. They were still capable, fools that they were, of repudiating everything he said and leading their country to destruction. They had no right to be here. There was not one of them fit to sit in the same room with him.

'We can take pride in our country,' he finished off abruptly, taunting them with their own disbelief, 'and pride in the community of which we are an essential part — the wider community that is Europe . . . that is civilization as we know it.'

Then he sat down.

The questions began to come. If one could call them questions. They were, rather, ammunition that had been stored up in readiness: amateurish jingoism, vicious slanders disguised as questions, mockery masquerading as the need for information.

None of them attacked the main principles of his case. How could they? He was right. He had always been right.

Time would show what fools they were. By then it might be too late. They had ears to hear and they would not hear. He would have to keep telling them, over and over and over again. But it would need a Hitler plus a Goebbels to do that and enforce it. Hitler and Goebbels were dead. Unworthy tools of a great cause, yet still bigger than any of their successors. He, Charles Tenby, was one of the few men of stature left in the world.

And they would not listen. The fools listened only to what they wanted to hear, not to the true meaning below.

He was handed a green card with the name of a visitor written on it. He was about to wave it away when he saw the name.

Sengall.

It was impossible. Sengall was dead. He had got rid of Sengall. Ghosts didn't come to the Houses of Parliament and fill in a visitor's card.

But he was caught up now in a dream where anything was possible. It must be a dream, suffused as it was with waves of irrational hatred rolling up from the shallows below him. The chatter of fools, reaching a pitch of madness. He had thought he belonged here in the House of Commons. How could he have been so blind? This was no place for him, no place for true men. If things had gone as they ought to have gone in 1939 the screeching, pecking birds would not have been savaging him like this. They would have chirped a more subdued tune then — a tune that he would have taught them.

He ought not to have been tempted; ought not to have forsaken the cause that was to have carried them to victory. Perhaps if he had stood firm the whole course of the war would have gone differently. He might by now have been in sole charge here, ordering these creatures rather than reasoning with them, establishing a sound régime which could last a thousand years . . .

It couldn't be Sengall out there.

But he had to see.

2

Tenby edged his way out. He received several frosty glances from his own back-benchers. Sooner or later they would have to learn a bitter, essential lesson. They all had so much, so very much, to learn.

Johnson was on his feet answering for the Government an irrelevant but complex question about tons of steel and convertor efficiency. The answer would be as hazy as the question but Johnson could be relied on to enjoy himself with it for some considerable time.

Tenby went along the echoing passage to the entrance hall. A young man turned to meet him.

It was the young thug who had broken into his home and stolen those documents.

Tenby said: 'I don't know whether you realize that it is a serious offence to put a false name on one of these cards.'

'The name isn't false. I'm Philip Sengall's son.'

In all his past dangers Tenby had never actually looked into the face of death. Now he knew that he was doing so.

He said: 'I can't imagine why you have come to see me.'

'You killed my father.'

'I have no idea what you are talking about. I may add that I have had quite enough of the criminal irresponsibility of Mr Evan Downing's employees. Sergeant . . . '

As he raised his arm the young man caught it. Tenby twisted away. A hand clamped down on his other arm, steadying him. He found General Henstock's face close to his own, the spattering of freckles almost scarlet against the livid skin.

'My dear chap . . . ' For once Tenby was glad to see Henstock. He steered him towards the green-carpeted stairs down to the restaurant and the bar as young Sengall was pulled back and held, struggling and arguing. Tenby hurried the general into the Strangers' Bar. Johnson's name still showed on the indicator. 'Delighted to see you. What will you have?'

'It was *you*!' Henstock's fury was so intense that the words came out scarcely above a whisper.

'You were upstairs while I was talking? I'd have got in touch with you earlier if

I'd had the chance. Unfortunately — '

'It was you,' said Henstock, 'and not Sengall after all.'

'I don't think you know what happened this weekend.'

'You sold us then' — Henstock's voice was rising — 'and you're doing it again. Your own skin — that's all you bloody well think about, isn't it?'

A scene like this in the bar would do no good at all. Tenby kept a tolerant smile on his lips as he urged the general towards the door and out on to the terrace. The air was biting and the sky above the river was a stony grey.

He said: 'All I could do inside was give an outline — '

'You little bastard. You wrecked everything for us. You looked after yourself years ago and now you're all set to play the same trick again. What do you think will happen when all those shares are dumped on the market? What do you think it'll mean to the rest of us when the news gets round? Do you even care? . . . Cheating, the way you cheated before . . . ' Henstock was screaming into Tenby's face.

Tenby had always hated that brutish mouth and the mottled cheeks. He wanted to brush Henstock aside with dignity, but heard himself saying: 'I did what I could for all of us. It wasn't only for me. Who got rid of Sengall? Not you. You tried and failed. *I* did it. You were a bungler. You were always a bungler.'

Henstock began to plod towards him, forcing Tenby back towards the wall of the terrace.

'It was you,' said Henstock over and over again. 'It was you. Not Sengall. It was you.'

Tenby's back was against the cold, hard wall. Henstock closed in and slammed a fist into his stomach. Tenby gasped and tried to writhe to one side. Henstock grabbed him and held him still while he smashed a fist into his face. Two men came running out of the bar but they appeared to move in slow motion, getting no nearer. Tenby jerked upwards away from the blows. He was taller than Henstock and tried to make himself taller still, vainly pushing himself up against the wall, almost climbing it backwards.

Henstock let out a delirious laugh. He lowered his head, butted Tenby in the chest, and got his arms round him. He lifted, sobbing and laughing at the same time, and Tenby's feet were off the ground. The wall was under the middle of his back. He began to sway to and fro, flailing his arms helplessly.

Henstock got one hand free, reached up, and put all his pressure on Tenby's neck.

It took only an instant of mad exertion. In that instant Henstock broke Tenby's back, heaved the body finally upwards, and let it slide limply over into the river.

3

Evan Downing said: 'You did a wonderful job.'

'You mean,' said Nora, 'that we provided you with some really big, horrible headlines for your front page.'

'Not only the front page,' said her uncle: 'we've got enough material to make feature articles for another week.'

'And after that it'll be dead?' said Alan.

'No story can be milked for ever,' said Downing regretfully.

Nora looked round the room. After the excitement of the last few weeks it looked very familiar and very normal. Wartime bombing had not shaken Viscount's Gate overmuch and there was no reason why recent events should have unsettled it. And Uncle Evan was, of course, the same as ever.

Alan Kershaw was not the man she had first met, so recently and yet so long ago. He was pale and somehow drained of energy, as though the sudden ending of their quest had robbed him of all that kept him going. The corners of his mouth were drawn down in a cynicism that she was now beginning to understand and share. Against her will she felt herself to be a part of him. His anger became her anger. That reckless plunge into Tenby's world had shown her what lay below the bland surface of England. Now she knew that she would see through Alan's eyes when she looked at the plump faces on television and in the newspapers, the smooth politicians and businessmen, the men who lived in a world where the unctuous interchange of Christian names blurred over a multitude of profitable sins.

Alan said indifferently: 'I suppose you'll have to handle this story with care. Henstock won't be in any position to get self-righteous, but there are others who can still have recourse to the law. The law.' There was despair in the repetition.

'What can be said outright will be said outright.' Downing might have been phrasing a public announcement. 'And when we cannot afford to be too direct . . . well, there are ways of leaking information. One does not need to shout. A well-directed whisper carries as far as one wishes it to go.'

Yes, said Nora mutely but clamorously to herself. Yes. Alan was right. He had been right all along about her uncle and all the others like him: all the experts who knew how to manipulate the great world of rumour in which news of births and marriages, swindles and divorces could be disseminated without risk if you knew the right means of communication.

'If we're in danger of being stymied,' said Downing, 'we can also fuss about setting up a public enquiry, until the Government have to agree to the formation of a tribunal. Then things come out — upside down or in the wrong order, but they come out. The tribunal's terms of reference don't matter: it's the seepage from behind the scenes that is so valuable. It worked during the Profumo business. It can be made to work again.'

Alan was studying Nora with a frightening, straight, serious expression that made her fumble for words. She made herself say:

'I'm beginning to see what you mean.'

He was immobile, unshaken, unresponsive. He seemed to be caught up in some icy trance.

'Tenby was right,' she said. 'That speech of his — you couldn't argue with his main assumptions. That's what is so awful. Half the time he was echoing your father. They could both be wrong. Or they could both be right. One had a profitable career and the other spent years in prison. Yet they both said precisely the same things.' This was the hideous mockery that dominated her thoughts. Sengall and Tenby were right about the world today; but since what they said today was what they had said in 1939, how could they have been wrong then? And if wrong then and for the next five years, how could they be right now? She thought of the Whepgate marchers, the snatches of conversation on the road, and before that the young man in Tenby's garden. Whom would it be dutiful to hate next when you were ordered to do so — the Chinese or the Russians or the Americans or the East Germans or the West Germans or the French or the South Africans or the Martians? . . . 'How do we get away?' she asked. 'You're the one who knows. You've been everywhere. I want to be where the air isn't contaminated by . . . by . . . '

Contaminated by the past, she wanted to say. But it would have been so pretentious.

Yet at the same time true. Futile millions had died in Flanders mud;

men had been pulped into slime in battle; women and children had been crushed in cellars and torn by broken glass while young German pilots flew homewards singing; women and children had been turned into human torches in the boiling Hamburg asphalt while Englishmen laughed and told dirty jokes and flew back to drink and tell more dirty jokes; the eyes of children lifted to the skies of Hiroshima had melted and run down their cheeks; and Uncle Evan was happy because he had material for a few sensational pages. Soon there would be Henstock's trial. Then there would be a big divorce case or a train smash or a rise in income tax.

She said: 'I want to leave here. I've come round to your viewpoint.'

'That's funny.' Alan laughed a dry laugh. 'Because I'm thinking of staying.'

'Glad to hear it,' said Evan Downing briskly. 'I want to talk to you. We can build up a wonderful authentic story around your experiences — about your life, the life in which you repudiated your father, and then the way you tracked down his killer as a matter of principle. A debt paid off . . . a fresh start. And then I'm prepared to give you a column of your own. What about that? Freedom to say just what you want. I promise. A new frank force in journalism — '

'As a stunt?' said Alan very quietly. 'In the hope of watching the rough edges rub off, Mr Downing? The expense account doing its work, the sharpness getting blunted?'

Nora was muzzily aware that she was going with Alan. She didn't know his destination, but she would be with him. He might try to shake her off . . .

He looked at her; and she knew that he was not going to shake her off.

She said: 'Alan . . . '

'Here we stay,' he said, 'and here we work. And whatever we do, we do it without Uncle Evan, the Papers.'

She was conscious of an answering gladness inside herself. She had been willing to abandon herself to whatever he wanted. She had been trying to tell herself that walking out of this country would solve all the problems or at least make it possible to leave them all behind; but really she had known that there was only one solution — or the beginnings of a solution.

She said tentatively: 'Where do we begin?'

'I wish I knew.'

Downing snorted. 'If you have any specific for saving the world you'll do better with the weight of a powerful newspaper behind you. However simple the answer may appear to you — '

'If it were simple,' said Alan, 'and if any one man could be certain of what needed doing, he'd be either a dictator or the saviour of mankind. Maybe both. After what we've gone through these last few weeks, I'm learning that there isn't likely to be any quick remedy. Walking away isn't a remedy, even for the one who does the walking.'

'So?' Downing prompted.

'So,' said Alan, 'we give a nudge here and apply pressure there. We wrestle with each problem as it arises.'

'Dear me. The inevitability of gradualness.

Fabian idealism and Liberal highminded-ness and enlightened pragmatism. It hasn't worked so far.'

'It has never been given the chance. And nothing else has worked. Nothing else is worth working *for*. If this fails, everything worth while fails.'

'We must add a brick wherever we can,' said Nora, 'and hope that one day it will all add up to . . . to a fortress.'

Alan pulled his chair closer and put his hand on hers. He began to laugh; and it was a rich, free, invigorating laugh. It blew away the stilted pomposity of what they had been saying and infused what remained with vitality and love.

He said: 'I never visualized myself as a bricklayer, but I suppose it's a more constructive thing to be than a rampaging bulldozer.'

When they got down to the job of transforming the fine symbols and analo-gies into reality it would sound less fine and prove more gruelling. High senti-ments needed deep foundations. But Nora laughed back at him and knew that they both meant to go on and that they would be happy together.

'Even the bulldozer,' she said, 'has its uses.'

His grip on her hand tightened. He said: 'When do we start?'

THE END

THE DARK BOATMAN

John Glasby

Five chilling tales: a family's history is traced back for four centuries — with no instance of a death recorded . . . The tale of an aunt who wanders out to the graveyard each night . . . A manor house is built on cursed land, perpetuating the evil started there long ago . . . The fate of a doctor, investigating the ravings of a man sent mad by the things he has witnessed . . . The evil residing at Dark Point lighthouse where the Devil himself was called up . . .

CASE OF THE DIXIE GHOSTS

A. A. Glynn

America's bloody Civil War is over, leaving a legacy of bitterness, intrigues and villainy — not all acted out on the American continent. A ship from the past docks in Liverpool, England; the mysterious Mr. Fortune, carrying a burden of secrets, slips ashore and disappears into the fogs of winter. And in London, detective Septimus Dacers finds that helping an American girl in distress plunges him into combat with the Dixie Ghosts, and brings him face-to-face with threatened murder — his own.

THE LONELY SHADOWS AND OTHER STORIES

John Glasby

The midnight moon rode high and the house seemed to transmute the moonlight into something terrible. The broken chimneys stretched up like hands to the heavens, the eyeless sockets of the windows staring intently along the twisting drive. On the floor of the library, strange cabalistic designs glowed with an eerie light and there was a flickering as of corpse candles — a cold radiance, a manifestation of the evil aura which had never left this place, instead crystallising inside its very walls . . .

THE MAN OUTSIDE

Donald Stuart

Working abroad, John Fordyce and his sister returned to England after learning that John was the beneficiary of the estate of his uncle, William Grant. Taking up occupancy of Raven House, a large mansion in its own grounds, they engaged servants to run it. But soon a series of mysterious events followed. A man was seen lurking around the house, and there had been an attempted break-in. Then the chauffeur was found in the library — stabbed to death . . .

THE DEVIL'S FOOTSTEPS

John Burke

From out of the bog alongside the ancient track to the fenland village of Hexney, a line of deep footprints ran, trodden into the dry surface of the abandoned droveway. Each night, the footprints advanced nearer to the village . . . When a young boy's body was found drowned in Peddar's Lode, the villagers' ire was directed at a stranger, Bronwen Powys. The mysterious Dr. Caspian becomes her ally, but they would soon be fighting for their very lives and souls . . .